"What you want, kid?"

"I-I wanted to sign up for the photography club."

The human buffaloes crammed into the desks gave a chorus of groans.

"Another nerd in the making," someone said.

"Let's have him for dinner," another said. "Put him out of his misery."

"Too right," somebody agreed. "Can't let them run free. They might multiply."

The older man turned back around and pointed with a finger so stubby it looked as if it was missing the last two joints. "Down at the back, through the machine room."

Martin fled.

T. DAVIS BUNN

CHARIOT
FAMILY PUBLISHING
*A Division of Cook
Communications Ministries*

Chariot Books™ is an imprint of Chariot Family Publishing
Cook Communications Ministries, Elgin, Illinois 60120
Cook Communications Ministries, Paris, Ontario
Kingsway Communications, Eastbourne, England

LIGHT AND SHADOW
© 1995 by T. Davis Bunn

Cover design by Foster Design
Cover photography by Gregory Halvorsen Schreck
First printing, 1995
Printed in the United States of America
99 98 97 96 95   5 4 3 2 1

This book is dedicated to
Cathy Davis
with heartfelt thanks for the
friendship and guidance,
and with the hopes that
her life to come
is filled with overflowing joy.

Martin pushed through the door marked Industrial Arts and entered bedlam.

Jock heaven, was what he thought, and he almost turned around. But the teacher heard the door thump closed and looked in his direction. Martin's eyes crawled upwards. The man had no forehead at all.

"Yeah?" the man barked. "What you want, kid?"

"I-I wanted to sign up for the photography club."

The human buffaloes crammed into the desks gave a chorus of groans.

"Another nerd in the making," someone said.

"Let's have him for dinner," another said. "Put him out of his misery."

"Too right," somebody agreed. "Can't let them run free. They might multiply."

The older man turned back around and pointed with a finger so stubby it looked as if it was missing the last two joints. "Down at the back, through the machine room."

Martin fled.

The door was not hard to find. It was covered with blow-ups and cut-outs of old pictures—art photographs cut from glossy magazines, with cruder attempts to copy the work pasted alongside.

There was a sign in the middle of the door which read, "If this door is closed, don't knock. If it's open, run for cover." Below someone had scribbled, "Caution: Nerds at work."

The door was cracked open. Martin knocked on a double exposure of a long-necked woman shadowed by a giraffe.

A voice from inside shouted, "Can't you read?"

Martin took one step back. "I just wanted—"

"Whatever it is you're selling," the voice shouted, "we're not buying."

"—to sign up for the photography club."

"Club?" The door flew open to reveal a boy who at first glance appeared to be a living puppet—all gangly limbs and awkward angles. He was over six feet tall and could not have weighed one hundred pounds. He was dressed entirely in black, from his sneakers to the bandanna around his forehead. "Who said anything about a club?"

Despite his best instincts, Martin held his ground. "The notice on the bulletin board."

"We're too exclusive to be a club." The gangly youth turned and asked somebody hidden inside, "What's more restricted than a club?"

"I dunno," replied a bored female voice from somewhere within. "Tell him the Marines are looking for a few good men."

"Right." The boy turned back around, pushed his glasses back up his nose, and asked, "So what's your name, kid?"

"Martin. Martin Powell."

"Okay, Martin. So here's the thing. I'm king of this super-club. You may address me as Your Highness."

The unseen girl inside made a rude noise.

"Silence, foul wench. This is supposed to be my lady-in-waiting, but I haven't promoted her yet because she hasn't learned to curtsey when I enter."

There was the sound of someone becoming violently ill. Martin bit back a smile.

"If we decide to accept you into our lofty ranks, you will be our slave."

"Now you're talking," the bored voice said.

"You will be the chief bottle washer, mess cleaner-upper, box carrier, wood splitter, and so on, and so forth."

"Just what I've always wanted," said the unseen girl. "My very own personal splitter of wood."

"You will also be the one dealing with Professor Cretin."

Martin blinked. "Who?"

"The man responsible for the animals foraging in the front room."

"Oh. Him."

"Yes, our very own throwback to the Neanderthal Age. His real name is Lynch. A perfect title for the football coach. Our regular Industrial Arts teacher retired two years ago. The school had another budget cutback, and so they put Lynch in charge of

IA. Which means that anything we need, we have to get from him."

"Which means," the bored voice said from within, "a constant battle."

"Which will be your responsibility," the gangly youth finished, and waited.

Martin shrugged. "Sounds okay."

"Okay, the man says." The youth cocked his head to one side. "You realize that you're consigning yourself to a fate worse than death."

"It's like an initiation, right?" Martin thought it over. "How hard can it be?"

"Hard," the girl's voice replied. "Note my gray hairs."

"I would if I could see you," Martin answered.

A girl almost as gangly as the guy and sporting a major-league nose poked her head through the doorway. She too wore a complete outfit of brilliant black. "See?"

"Horrors," Martin said. "Where do I sign?"

"Not so fast. First comes the examination." His Highness reached inside the room, turned back around, held out his hand, and said, "What am I holding?"

Martin looked for the gimmick, found none. "A camera."

"Okay, you pass. And now the selection committee will meet." He looked down at his sidekick. "How many applied for the position of slave?"

The dark-haired girl cocked a thumb at Martin. "You're looking at him."

"See?" The tall boy was exceedingly smug. "Super exclusive. So special nobody even tried to join up."

The would-be lady-in-waiting rolled her eyes and said, "All in favor of appointing Martin slave-for-the-year say aye."

"Yo."

"All opposed?"

"You realize," the gangly youth warned one last time, "dealing with Professor Cretin means running the jock gauntlet at least once a week. They all gather down here for homeroom. Lynch has some theory about developing team spirit. So when you want to ask him for something, which he only lets you do before or after school, you've either got to do it here or out on the field."

"Not fun," the dark-haired girl warned. "Not fun at all."

"But we both did it our first years and survived," the gangly youth added. "So what do you say?"

"Count me in."

"Right." He stuck out his hand. "Floyd Weathers. And this is Ellen Ferguson." The boy lowered his head. "Also known as mine. Got it?"

Ellen offered her hand and said in ever-weary cynicism, "Welcome to Pandemonium."

"The school puts up with us only because we're cheaper than an outside photographer," Floyd explained.

"One senior, one junior, one sophomore," Ellen added. "That's the quota."

They were squeezed inside the darkroom, which was nothing more than an oversized windowless closet. Two broad shelves ran down the side walls, with sinks set midway in both. Plastic trays sat in crowded rows. Narrow shelves crammed with chemicals and boxes climbed the walls. Overhead ran clotheslines, empty save for two strings of negatives. At the back wall was a tall machine with an accordion neck pointed down at a glass-topped surface.

Martin thought it was the neatest place he'd ever seen.

"But in return for the trickle of stuff we squeeze out of Neander-man," Floyd went on, "we've got to take all the photographs for the yearbook and the school rag. Which means somebody has to go to every football game, basketball game, sock hop, theater, orchestra, student government assembly, blah, blah, blah."

"Beyond boring," Ellen said.

"Time away from the real stuff," Floyd agreed.

"Which is?" Martin asked.

"Art," Floyd said.

"Avant-garde," Ellen added. "Post Modernism. The cutting edge of photography. Where the world is pointed."

"We're headed for the big time," Floyd said. "Weathers and Ferguson, the dream team. Mark my words, Peon. One day you'll look back and say with pride, I knew them when."

"I think it would be kind of nice to take pictures of the school stuff," Martin confessed.

That brought a jaw-dropping silence. "I must be dreaming," Floyd declared.

"If I am," Ellen replied, "don't you dare wake me."

"Did I say something wrong?" Martin asked.

"No, no, no, far from it. You're the perfect peon."

"If he can take pictures," Ellen corrected.

"Yeah, that's right. Do you know your way around cameras?"

"A little," Martin replied. "I've always liked shooting pictures. I've got an old Minolta that was . . ." Martin stopped and swallowed hard, "my dad's. But it's broken."

If they noticed his hesitation they made no sign. "Shame it's broken," Ellen said.

"That's right. You see, Peon, this darkroom is sadly lacking."

"Woefully," Ellen agreed. "Outrageously. Criminally."

Floyd glared her way. "I'll choose the adjectives around here."

"Sorry, Your Highness."

"Right." He turned back to Martin. "We don't even have a developer for color film. Which means that either we work with black-and-white—"

"Which is definitely past tense," Ellen interrupted. "Over the hill. Strictly bogusville."

"—Or we have to take our film to a local shop," Floyd went on. "Which means paying too much, as far as the school is concerned."

"Two cents is too much as far as the school's concerned," Ellen explained. "Especially since most of the shots they use in the yearbook and everything in the school newspaper"—she paused to make a gagging sound—"has to be in black-and-white."

"But our art is in color," Floyd replied.

"I think I see," Martin said.

"Of course you do," Floyd said, patting him on

the head. "You're an intelligent peon."

"But there are also other things we're missing," Ellen said. "Such as telephoto lenses for our one and only autofocus camera."

"Which is the exclusive property of the great and glorious senior member of this clan," Floyd said. "Namely me."

Ellen stuck out her tongue. "And only one other thirty-five millimeter camera, which I've got dibs on."

"Which leaves the dinosaurs for our new peon," Floyd said. He reached to a high shelf and pulled down a couple of ancient-looking cameras. He pretended to blow off the dust and handed them over. "Take your pick."

They were battered and ugly and heavy as lead. Martin looked at them doubtfully. "Thanks, I guess."

"Football season starts in three weeks," Floyd announced with relish. "That should give you enough time to get acquainted with your new friends. Any questions and all that." He looked down at his dark-haired sidekick. "Okay, go get our new peon a key."

Ellen disappeared and returned in a flash. She dangled the key in front of his face, and said in her best teacherlike voice, "Have fun, dear."

Martin had his mother's dark hair and his father's light gray eyes. He was not a big person. In fact, he was small for his age, although his mother refused to let him say the word. She called him compact. Martin thought that was worse. It sounded like the kind of car he had to fold his knees up under his chin to enter.

His father had been slim and undersized, and his mother two inches shorter than his father, so Martin did not have any great expectations of growing much bigger. All he could hope for was strong, and even that hope did not go too far. He had a set of barbells in his room and a chin-up bar strung in his doorway, and he worked out with them every morning and evening. But he had long since stopped measuring his height and chest and arms the way his father had told him to do when he had given Martin the set. The measurements never changed.

Martin told his mother about signing up with the photography club over dinner that night. "Those two are a real pair," he finished. "But I think maybe it'll be fun."

"Jack would be very pleased to hear that you've taken up photography," she replied.

Martin didn't know what to say to that. Jack was his father. He had been an engineer. He had died of a heart attack the year before. When his mother talked about him in that way, as though he were still alive and had just stepped out for a while, it always left Martin feeling as if a wound had opened in his heart.

His mother's name was Margaret, but everybody called her Marge. Not Maggie. She hated that name. She said it sounded like a name somebody would give a very slow dog. Marge was anything but slow. She was dark and slender and full of energy. She was a nurse, and had coped with her husband's death in her normal matter-of-fact way, accepting the sorrow and the tears and then putting them away.

For Martin it had been much harder. And every time his mother spoke of her husband in that calm way, it left Martin feeling as though it had all happened last week, instead of last year.

He covered his discomfort by going up to his room for the two cameras. They looked even worse away from the darkroom's surroundings. He brought them back downstairs and showed them to his mother. "They say I've got to use these."

Marge inspected them. "They don't look like much, do they?"

Martin shook his head. "And both of them show everything upside down."

Marge began gathering dinner plates. "I know what Jack would say."

Again there was that blooming of pain. "What?"

"He'd say, 'If life's dealt you a pile of rocks, go out and build yourself a house.' "

Everything about high school was different.

Martin walked the campus, still trying to keep from getting lost between classes. The halls seemed endless, the other students, giants. And he did not know anyone. Not a soul.

Moving to the other side of town had been part of Marge's way of dealing with her loss. She had taken a different job at a new hospital, found them a small townhouse in a new development, and enrolled him at Westover High. At the time, Martin had been too busy adjusting to life without his father to complain.

Now he wasn't so sure keeping quiet had been the right thing to do.

As the fog of sorrow cleared, Martin found himself completely alone. His mother was kept permanently busy trying to manage a household by herself and work a very demanding job. His friends were all the way across town, and over the summer he had watched them gradually drift away. They were entering a different high school and were busy with activities that no longer had a place for him.

And he missed his father more than he thought possible.

Jack Powell had been a quiet, bespectacled man with a surprising amount of strength hidden within his spare frame. He had never been tremendously affectionate, but he had always treated Martin as a friend as well as a son. His sudden departure left a gaping hole in Martin's life.

Martin filled it the only way he knew how, with constant activity. Which was the real reason behind his joining the photography club. Such as it was.

The next afternoon he lugged the cameras outside to where the football team was practicing. Coach Lynch saw him and waved him over. "What're you doing here?"

"I'm supposed to take pictures of the games," Martin replied. "I thought I might as well get some practice in too."

Coach Lynch really was an astonishing sight. His head sort of caved in towards the front, reducing his forehead to a narrow slant. His nose was flattened close to his face, and his jaw was as square as a brick. His features looked as craggy and seamed as old sneakers. "This is supposed to be a closed practice," he said doubtfully. "But I guess it's okay."

"Thanks," Martin said, and backed off before he could change his mind.

Sighting pictures of fast-moving players who ran upside down through the viewfinder was harder than Martin expected. Not to mention the fact that the cameras were so heavy that it was tough to keep them upright. Martin spent an hour firing picture after picture without any film, just trying to get everything straight. He learned that he had to begin tracking a player long before the shot, holding the camera with one hand while operating the focus ring with the other. Then at the precise moment he had to click the shutter. All while aiming at a boy running on his helmet across a blue ground flecked with clouds.

The one thing which surprised him was how clear it all looked through the viewfinder. Sometimes he would take his eye away from the camera, look around, and feel a sort of shadow dimming everything. The view through the camera was crystal clear. If only it could be right side up.

"You're handling that Graflex like a real pro," said a quaky voice.

Martin started at the unexpected sound. He lowered the camera and saw a frail old man leaning heavily on a cane. "What?"

"A Graflex is one heavy sucker to cart around. Especially for action shots." The old man's eyes were the only bright part about him. "You must be dry-firing it. I haven't seen you change the film."

"I was just practicing," Martin said, for some reason feeling he needed to defend himself. "Today's the first time I ever used it."

"Then you've got the hands of a natural," the old man said. He shifted the cane to his other hand and reached out his free hand. "Here, let me show you something."

Reluctantly, Martin handed him the camera, but the old man did not take it. Instead he grasped Martin's wrist. His fingers were covered with the dry parchment-like skin of the elderly. Martin allowed his hand to be guided through what he had thought was just a carry strap. Then the old man tightened the strap until Martin's hand was pressed up tight against the camera body. His fingers curved naturally around a leather grip he had not even noticed before. And all of a sudden the camera was no longer clumsy.

"Hey, it balances!"

"A natural, just as I said." The old man pointed at Martin's other arm. His finger shook slightly as he did so. "That leaves your right hand free to handle the light meter, focus, and shoot."

Martin turned and focused on a player going for a long pass. "If only you could make the images right side up."

"What you are seeing," the old man replied, "is the exact image that is being placed upon the film. Not a millimeter more or less. When the Graflex was designed, that in itself was a real breakthrough. There is a prism inside the camera, you see, which splits the image entering through the focal lens. One half goes to the film, the other to your eye. For a professional photographer, being able to know exactly what would appear on the film was much more important than adapting to a reversed image."

A reversed image. This man really knew his stuff. Martin picked up the other camera at his feet. "And this one?"

"Ah, the early Hasselblad. The finest hand-ground lenses ever made. This one requires you to bend over and focus while looking down, which means it is normally used for stills. That is, shots which you can set up." Shaky fingers reached out and flicked open the viewfinder, which sprang up from the top like an empty jack-in-the-box. "But the image you see is exactly the size of the image on the film. Again, a tremendous advantage for precise focusing. This and the lens quality means that more professional portrait photographers use Hasselblads than any other camera in the world."

"When they gave me these cameras they made it sound like a punishment detail."

"They?"

"The other members of the photography club."

The old man showed his distaste. "I suppose the others are using the thirty-five-millimeter apparatus."

Martin nodded. "Autofocus and everything."

"There are advantages to the new cameras," the old man replied. "But some vital lessons can only be learned on cameras such as these. The fact that they are not automatic means that you must learn to be extremely careful. You must set up every shot. You must be prepared, and you must wait." The old eyes were a frosty blue, and held a brilliance which belied the man's years. "You will learn patience with these cameras. And skill. Then you can move on to the more modern cameras with your talents deepened in ways that would never otherwise have been possible."

Martin eyed the old man with astonishment. "How do you know all this?"

"My name is Carruthers," the old man replied. "Until two years ago I taught here at Westover High."

You slide the film plate in like this," Mr. Carruthers said, demonstrating with swift, practiced motions. "Then you flick this little switch, pull out the protective sleeve, and you're ready to shoot." He replaced the sleeve, then handed Martin both the camera and the light meter. "All right, now you try it from the beginning."

Martin fumbled with the unfamiliar apparatus. "I need another hand."

"Sling the light meter around your neck. That's it. All right, now, take Helen's picture."

"Don't you dare," Mrs. Carruthers said sharply. "I'm still in my housedress. Do you take milk or lemon with your tea, dear?"

"Uh, lemon," Martin guessed, never having had hot tea before. He watched Mrs. Carruthers pour out a steaming cup and set it down in front of him. She had called him "dear" since the moment he had entered the house. "Thank you."

"You're most welcome, dear. Now help yourself to the cookies. And please keep an eye on Harold. The doctor has told him he is supposed to avoid sugar, but when it comes to cookies I might as well be dealing with a nine-year-old child."

Mr. Carruthers harrumphed and said, "I think we can manage things very well from here, Helen."

Mrs. Carruthers straightened and smiled at Martin. "Are you a photographer, dear?"

"I'd like to be." Martin lifted his cup and took a cautious sip. It tasted almost as good as it smelled.

"How nice. Well, you must be sure and come visit us often. This house has been far too empty since Harold retired."

"Helen," Mr. Carruthers repeated.

"Oh, his old students come by every now and then," she went on, ignoring her husband's impatience. "A number of their pictures hang in the living room and down the hall. But it's not the same, don't you know. They are all so busy with their own lives that they come and they go, whoosh, moving like the wind."

"I'd like to see them," Martin said. "The pictures, I mean."

"Yes, Harold has quite a number of former students who are now professionals. And how many have won national awards, is it seven or eight?"

"I'm sure I don't remember," Mr. Carruthers said testily. "Now if you'll excuse—"

"Harold has a gift for teaching, you see. We were never blessed with children ourselves, but I have always considered Harold's special pupils to be a part of our family." Her smile was full of a genuine warmth. "You must have something quite special, you know, dear. Harold only brings home students who have a special talent."

"He's never even seen any of my pictures," Martin protested, falling into the older lady's habit of talking about her husband as though he were not in the room.

"Oh, that doesn't matter. How Harold manages to pick them out is a wonder. Perhaps by smell. But he's almost always right." She reached down and patted Martin's cheek with a hand as frail as autumn leaves. "I'm sure you are quite special, dear. You have the look about you. Don't you think so, Harold?"

Her husband muttered something inaudible and noisily slurped at his tea.

"Well, you must have a lot you want to discuss, so I'll just go sit myself down in the living room. Be sure and let me know if you need anything." With that she bustled away.

Mr. Carruthers gave an exasperated sigh and mouthed the word, "Finally."

"All right," he said out loud. "Now I want you to try and photograph the bowl of fruit on the dining table over there. No, no, wait a moment, don't start with your camera," he cautioned, when Martin stood and began focusing. "That comes last. First you must calculate the light with your meter."

"I don't see why I need to worry about that," Martin protested, "when new cameras do all that stuff automatically."

"Indeed they do," Mr. Carruthers agreed. "But

what if you wish to photograph sunlight through leaves? How can you be sure that your camera is metering for the leaves and not the naked light? Or what if you are trying for a softer image? How can you adjust for this, if you don't understand the basics underlying your trade?"

"I think I see," Martin said.

"Photography is like life," Mr. Carruthers said. "In order to be successful, you must build on a solid foundation." He pointed at where sunlight came through the window and landed on the table. "Now position the bowl so that it rests in the light. Then I want you to try and see with the camera's eye. Remember, you are working with black-and-white film, so color does not matter. Here again you are going back to the very bedrock of picture making. You are stripping away color, and trying to make a picture out of light and shadow alone."

Light and shadow. Martin spent the next five days feeling like a total fool, but doing as the old man had instructed. Every day after school he lugged the cameras into his backyard, where he set up a bowl of fruit on a picnic table and began taking pictures. Real pictures. Using real film. The old man had said it was necessary for him to begin shooting with film.

"How long will I have to keep doing this?" Martin had asked.

"Until you start having a feel for light and shadow alone," Mr. Carruthers had replied.

"How long will that be?" Martin had demanded.

The old man had smiled and replied simply, "You will know."

Martin walked around and around and around the table, feeling totally foolish, very glad that the tall fence kept his neighbors from seeing him.

On the second day he had a fleeting vision of trying to explain what he was doing to Floyd and Ellen, and almost gave up. But something inside him rebelled at being a quitter this early in the game. So on he went.

On the third day a sudden rain squall drove him indoors. An hour later the sun reappeared. Martin went outside to find the fruit sparkling with raindrops. He angled his shot so as to have the sunlight reflected up through the water, like thousands of little prisms. That evening he went back indoors feeling that maybe he was getting somewhere.

On the fourth day he got nowhere fast, and quit in a sullen rage.

On the fifth day it all came together.

It was Saturday, so Martin began earlier than usual, utterly glum at the thought that he had nothing better to do with his free day than take pictures of a bowl of fruit.

Maybe it was because the angle of morning sun was different. Maybe it was because he did not have school that day, and so he was fresher than usual. Maybe the practice had worn him down enough that he was able to look at things differently. Whatever the reason, after Martin had been at it for an hour or so, he looked through the viewfinder and he *saw*.

A line of shadow from the back fence cut off the top third of the bowl. It looked like a moon-shaped sea of black. In the middle of this darkness, an apple was just high enough for its top surface to rise up like a circular island. Martin pushed the bowl back farther, and saw how the shadows swallowed up the rest of the bowl's depths. He took out all but three pieces of fruit, and arranged them so that they were set equidistant around the bowl. He looked through the viewfinder, and saw three tiny circular islands in a dark circular sea. He took a picture, and this time he knew it was going to be good.

He straightened back up, and for the first time noticed the shadow of a tree angling in from the corner of the yard. Martin set the bowl of fruit on the ground, and shifted the table over so that one shadow branch fell on it. He twisted the table around so that it cleaved the table in two, running from corner to corner. He could not explain why, but the lines of shadow seemed to form a tension on the tabletop, as though the shadow lines were in tight conflict with the table. He took another picture.

Then he decided the table was too dark to form the sort of contrast he wanted. He started to go inside for a white tablecloth, then stopped. He set down the camera and light meter, went to the outdoor faucet, and came back with a double handful of water. He splashed it over the table. Martin looked down and felt the thrill of discovery. The water disrupted the shadow, curving it out in places, and somehow accented the tension between shadow and reality. He moved around the table, and found the point where the sun shot back up towards him through the water and formed little rainbows.

With one hand he began sweeping away all the water that did not lie directly along the shadow's path. Then he took the cloth he used to clean the lenses, and wiped all the table dry except for where the shadow fell. He picked up the camera, looked through the viewfinder, and shivered.

The shadow surface was curved and bumpy, just like a real tree limb. And where the outer edges met the sunlight, the water drops were transformed to thousands and thousands of tiny jewels. The shadow tree had grown leaves of light.

Martin shot a couple of pictures, then a voice behind him said, "Do you realize you've been standing out here for over three hours?"

The sound made him jump so high both feet left the ground. He whirled around to find his mother watching him with her arms crossed over her chest. She demanded, "What on earth are you doing?"

"Learning to work with light and shadow," he replied, knowing it sounded feeble.

"Is this a school project?"

"Sort of." For some reason he had found himself reluctant to talk about Mr. Carruthers.

"You were really caught up in it, whatever it was you were doing." She looked at him oddly. "You really like this photography business, don't you?"

He nodded. "It's a lot more challenging than I thought."

"Your father had the same ability to concentrate."

"I remember." He did, and with the same old pain.

But Marge was too busy with her own memories to notice Martin's reactions. "When he was working on something, or reading some book he liked, I could walk through the room, carry on a conversation, stand on my head in the corner, and he wouldn't even notice. I never met anyone . . ." Marge stopped and bit her lip. She took a deep breath, then said, "I have to go to work. Your lunch is on the table."

"All right," Martin said, but he was distracted by an idea taking form in his mind.

She walked over, mussed his hair, and kissed him. "I miss your father," she confessed.

"So do I," he said quietly, still dwelling in the image he saw with his mind's eye.

"Sometimes you remind me so much of him," she said. "It helps and it hurts at the same time. Like talking about him. Do you know what I mean?"

"Yes," he said, and this time he could hear her talk like that and not become lost in his own pain, because somehow the image in his mind was giving shape to his pain.

"I won't be too late," she said, and turned away. "Call if you need anything."

As soon as she had left, Martin raced upstairs to the attic. It was the first time he had been up there since they had moved in. Even during the move itself, Martin had avoided looking at the boxes that held his father's things. Now he pulled away boxes, feeling the pain blossom inside his chest, and yet knowing it was all right. Not understanding why, but knowing just the same.

And the knowing was enough.

When he had found what he was looking for, he raced downstairs. In the utility room he found an old sheet his mother was going to tear up for rags. Then back upstairs to his room for a felt-tipped pen. He tore down the stairs and out the door, and knew a moment's keen relief when he saw the sun was still there. The desire to make his image real had become so strong that for a moment he had actually become frightened of clouds arriving and blocking the light.

Martin spread the sheet out on the table, then set his father's eyeglasses on the covering. He shifted the glasses around until the shadow was clearest, forming almost a twin of the complete spectacles.

He uncapped the felt pen and began drawing tears falling down the covering from the shadow glasses. He worked as fast as he could, knowing the sun would soon alter its position so much that the picture would be lost. When he had ten tears falling from each shadow-lens, he picked up the light meter and took a fast reading. Then he lifted the camera, set the aperture and speed, and looked through the viewfinder.

The power of what he had done hit him hard. The actual eyeglasses were important only because they formed a shadow. The shadow glasses seemed more real, especially when he angled the camera so that the real glasses were shoved up to the far left corner of the frame.

The shadow glasses cried shadow tears. A man who was not there wept for a son he could not see. A boy who would become a man the shadow glasses would never see grow up. A boy who would grow up without the father who now was only a shadow.

Martin had trouble taking the picture because of the tears that filled his own eyes.

When he arrived at the Carrutherses' house the next day, he did not receive the greeting he expected.

"Oh, Martin, hello," Mrs. Carruthers said, but her smile was somewhat distracted, and she did not invite him in. "I'm not sure . . . well, you see, Harold likes to spend his sabbath afternoons alone with God. I'm sure you understand."

"Yes," Martin replied, not understanding in the least.

"You could come back this evening if you like. Or perhaps I could pass on a message."

"Tell him," Martin said, pushing through the emotions which were crowding up inside, "tell him I think I'm beginning to understand."

"How nice. Now you just sit yourself down there on the swing while I go see if he has any reply. Wait right there." And with that she closed the screen door and walked away.

Martin settled himself into the swing hanging from one end of the long front porch. Theirs was an old wooden house, with white pillars holding up an overhanging roof, and wisteria clinging to the eaves. It was a comfortable house, scuffed and faded around the edges, but made beautiful with the memories that whispered at him where he sat.

Mrs. Carruthers opened the screen door and said, "Harold says that you should go and combine motion with what you have learned. You are to work on this for a week, and then come over next Saturday. Does that make any sense to you, dear?"

Martin mulled it over and decided, "I think so."

"Well, that's fine, because I couldn't make heads nor tails of it, and so I made him repeat it three times, which he hates doing. But there you are. Now you go off and enjoy your sabbath, dear, and be sure to come back again soon."

Monday afternoon he went back to the darkroom, and was immensely glad to find that Floyd and Ellen were not there. He was not yet ready to confess that he had been taking instruction from a retired high school teacher and had spent the week shooting a bowl of fruit.

But there was a note waiting for him.

Dear Peon,

Your duties include cleaning house every Friday, which you missed. Don't let it happen again, under threat of being disbarred or dismembered or disarmed, take your pick. Hope you're busy getting the hang of your gear, as I have already promised Coach Lynch that you will

be shooting our great and glorious team in action.
You have two weeks left.

Love and all that,
King Floyd

Martin found a bucket and rags at the back of the room, and got busy. When he was fishing out papers and trash scattered around the floor, he discovered a battered old case crammed under the sink. He pulled it out, worked the rusted clasps, and opened the lid.

Inside were revealed a couple of old dog-eared books, one on the Hasselblad and one on the Graflex. There was also a canvas shoulder strap, an extra light meter, boxes of negatives which had long passed their expiration dates, and another half-dozen film-plates for the Graflex. There were also a series of filters and additional lenses set into tight little built-in holders, a tripod, a flash apparatus for each camera, and three boxes of bulbs. Along one side were two cavities into which the Graflex and Hasselblad and the second light-meter could fit snugly.

Martin felt as though he had just discovered Aladdin's cave.

But carrying the box when fully loaded was another story.

By the time he had made it from the school to the far field where the football team was practicing, Martin felt as if the canvas strap had dug a trough in his shoulder. He arrived at the sidelines, set the case down, and straightened slow and easy. His shoulder throbbed.

Coach Lynch walked over. "Floyd tells me you're gonna be shooting the games this year."

"Yessir."

"Used to be, only the seniors were allowed to handle that responsibility," Coach Lynch said doubtfully. "Sure you can do it?"

Martin tried to hide his own doubts. "I think so. I'll try hard."

"Well, that'll sure make a change from those other two," the coach said, still not convinced. "They act like shooting pictures of my boys is about as exciting as an evening at the local morgue."

"I like football," Martin assured him.

"That'll help, I guess," the coach said, his perpetual scowl not easing. "Just promise me that if you're not getting any decent pictures, you won't wait until after the season's over to tell somebody."

"No problem."

"A lot of these guys wait all year to see themselves in the yearbook. We don't want to disappoint them, you know what I mean?"

"Yes." Martin lifted his camera. "Is it okay if I take some more practice shots?"

The coach sighed, shook his head. "Yeah, I guess so. Just stay outta the way." With that he turned and stomped back towards the players, yelling and pointing as he went.

Martin swiftly discovered that all the practice of the week before really helped. The light meter no longer took minutes to read and calculate. The camera did not feel so clumsy in his hands. His motions were becoming smoother.

The Graflex used a massive negative. Each film

measured three and one-quarter inches by four and one-quarter inches, bigger than his hand. They were held on flat glass plates that slid in and out of the back of the camera. When the negative plate was set in place and he was ready to take the picture, Martin first had to pull out the protective sleeve, a thin metal sheet which fitted over the negative and protected it from light. After the picture was taken, Martin slid the protective sheet back into place, then pulled out the big negative plate, flipped it over, and stuck it back into the camera. Then the second negative, which was on the reverse side of the plate from the first, could be taken. But only after its protective sleeve was taken out.

It was all tremendously complicated.

Making it worse was his need to first use the light meter to take a reading on how much sunlight there was. Then he had to calculate the camera's aperture, or the width of the lens hole through which light passed. The aperture settings were called *f*-stops, and acted like a funnel permitting light back onto the negative. The shutter speed was then set, to determine how long the funnel would be open to let in the light.

Then of course there was the negative's own light sensitivity to factor in. Along with a dozen other things which Martin was only beginning to understand.

Light and shadow. Aperture and shutter speed. Focus. Making sure the negative was in place and the protective sleeve slipped out.

And now motion.

Martin stationed himself on the sidelines so that the sun was behind him. He then took a careful reading with the light meter. He took out a negative plate, checked carefully to make sure it had not been used before, slid it into the back of the camera, and removed the protective sleeve.

He was ready.

Kevin Murphy, quarterback, school hunk. After fewer than four weeks of high school, even Martin knew that. Martin had seen Kevin walk the halls, ever in the company of the school bombshell, Nancy Starling. His dark good looks were perfectly complemented by Nancy's classic blond complexion. Martin had slowed several times to watch them pass, heaving great internal sighs of longing.

Martin decided to focus on Kevin, both because he was the natural center of attention and because it was easier to plan shots if he had one particular person in mind. It all moved so fast.

That day he shot twenty photos, all the negatives he had. When that was over, he stayed around, continuing to focus and shoot and watch. Always watching.

It was as close as he had ever come to feeling a part of the game.

The next day he arrived while the team was still busy with their calisthenics. Coach Lynch scowled in his direction and growled something, but he didn't come over. The day after that it rained, so Martin spent the time reading the two books he had found in the darkroom and changing the negative plates. Putting new film on the plates was harder than he thought, since it had to be done in total darkness. The used film was stored in a plastic case called the development tank. The new film had to be put in by feel alone. But as the book said, the film had one side which was slicker than the other. The slick side went face-up, because it had the chemicals to catch the light and make the picture. By the time Martin had changed all twenty plates he was sweating hard.

Thursday was cloudy and dull. He was not too disappointed when he stopped by his locker after lunch to find a note from Floyd.

School rag meeting this afternoon, Room 303.
Be there.

His Royal Highness

Someone—Martin assumed it was Ellen—had crossed out the last word and written, "Dunderhead."

Miss Paisley was someone Martin classed as permanently flustered. Her brown hair was caught in an untidy bun. Her glasses were always skewed to one side. She spoke in sort of breathless catches while her brown eyes voiced a mute appeal. Martin liked her on sight.

"Oh, well, Martin. How nice. . . ." Miss Paisley waved him towards any of the free seats. "Class, Martin Powell will take pictures for us, I think, that is, yes."

"That is," finished a curly-haired boy sprawled in the back row, "unless he's as big a pain as our terrible twins."

"Class, please."

"Getting pictures from those two," declared an auburn-haired girl with bottle-bottom glasses, "was about as much fun as a trip to the dentist."

"Janice, what will Martin think?" Miss Paisley gave her frayed hairdo a nervous pat.

Martin chose the desk next to the girl named Janice, who said, "Mind if I ask you something?"

"Shoot."

"Are you planning to actually work with us? I mean, the idea of having a school photographer is for somebody to be there and take photographs of school events. Or am I just being totally naive?"

"Sounds about right to me."

That brought an astonished silence. Miss Paisley broke it with, "You mean, you will attend the games?"

Martin shrugged. "Sure."

Janice demanded, "And take pictures of people when we ask?"

Martin shrugged. "Why not?"

A boy at the back of the room said, "Amazing."

"I must say, Martin," Miss Paisley pushed up her glasses, "this is, well, rather . . ."

"Try incredible," Janice offered.

"I'll believe it when I see it," the boy at the back of the room said.

Janice demanded, "You're not after the world's best close-up photograph of a fingernail?"

"No."

"Or a smoking gun spouting from a water faucet?"

Martin shook his head.

"How about a black rainbow in a green sky?" Janice asked.

Martin laughed.

Janice exchanged looks with Miss Paisley, then said, "Am I giving you an idea of the kind of stuff those two expected us to stick in the newspaper? Like when we wanted a picture of the principal, who we will all agree is not the world's most brilliant photographic material—"

"Janice, please," Miss Paisley said, glancing nervously at the door.

"—giving an award to one of the students, and what do we get but a picture of the principal growing purple and green spots, his arms out ready to hug a hippopotamus."

"Crocodile," someone corrected.

"Whatever." Janice eyed him through glasses so thick it made her eyes swim in murky depths. "I mean, high-class journalism it's not, but it is our school newspaper. And we sometimes need pictures. Is that asking too much?"

"Like for next week's rag," someone added.

"Right," Janice agreed. "We've got a football issue coming out. Can you get us something?"

Martin stood and moved for the door. "I'll see what I can do."

Friday dawned clear and chilly, the first real autumn day. After school Martin first cleaned the darkroom, then carried the heavy camera case out to the practice field. He set up again with the sun behind him, so that the light would be clearest for his pictures.

He was learning many things without conscious awareness of his progress. Like this time, he saw that in order to make a decent picture, he was going to need to find some way of separating the central figure from the pack. Otherwise it would be just one more body in a group, all of whom were dressed exactly the same. There weren't even faces to distinguish them, since everybody wore helmets. Just uniforms and padding and helmets and numbers.

"Okay!" shouted Coach Lynch from the sidelines. "Let's run through those pass plays! Get a move on!"

Coach Lynch was always shouting, so Martin rarely paid him any mind. But this time an alarm went off. Martin closed the box, heaved it to his shoulder, and ran farther downfield.

Martin dropped his case, did a quick check with the light meter, slid in a new photographic plate, and hefted the camera. By now he was able to set the picture without too much thought to the fact that the image was upside down.

One of the players detached himself and ran down field. Martin watched and tried to frame the shot. It was difficult, because the focus had to be constantly adjusted as the player moved closer. He shot several pass plays, but the motion was so fast from this angle that he feared none of them would turn out.

Then he remembered something he had read in the book the night before. Something about f-stop settings. Martin opened the case, pulled out the book, and thumbed the pages. There it was. "The higher the *f*-stop, the smaller the aperture. The smaller the aperture, the greater the field of focus." At the time, the words had meant nothing. But now, Martin saw that if he closed down the aperture, the range of field in focus was much greater. He checked the chart and saw that at the largest *f*-stop of 36, everything from three feet all the way out to infinity would be in focus. He would have to shoot at a slower speed, but with so much sunlight that really didn't matter. Great.

Only the pass plays run down his side of the field worked. Otherwise the players were too far away. Martin moved closer to the sideline and waited. Each time a player broke downfield on his side, he raised the camera and tried to keep him in focus, but not worrying about it too much, more just trying to frame a good shot.

He missed more than he made. A lot more. Sometimes he waited too long for the shot, until the player had made the catch and turned around. Or the player dropped the ball. Or the player ran and jinked to one side or another, and Martin didn't follow the move. After awhile, though, he was able to anticipate the moves, but it cost him a lot of time and film. Before he knew it, Martin was down to his last four negatives.

He set himself in a direct angle to where most of the passes were sent, determined to make this a good shot. Then he waited. Finally the player whom Coach Lynch called the tight end pushed past the blockers and sprinted right towards him. Martin raised the camera. He shifted slightly to one side so that he could see the quarterback in the background. Like a dozen times before, the player jinked right just at the same spot. The ball was in the air. Martin crouched, and shot. Click. The player caught the ball, turned, and barreled straight up the sideline for the end zone.

And hammered straight into Martin.

Martin had just enough time to raise the camera out of the line of impact. Which meant he caught the player's shoulder straight in his chest. And the helmet on the side of his head.

Martin saw stars. His breath went out with a *whoof!* He slid back ten yards on the grass, pinned to the ground by the player lying on top of him.

The player bounded up, furious. "What the heck are you doing, man? You messed up a totally good play!"

Martin was too busy trying to gulp in a little air to reply.

Coach Lynch came racing up. "You all right, Horner?"

The player slammed the ball down on the ground. "The best catch I made all day, and what happens but a nerd photographer gets in my way."

Coach Lynch turned and glared down at Martin. "I said you could hang around as long as you didn't get in the way. Just be glad this didn't happen in a game, son, or I'd have torn you into little pieces. Now get off my playing field!"

Martin rolled over with a groan. The side of his head felt like it had been partially separated from the rest of his body.

A pair of cleats moved into view. "I haven't finished with you yet, nerd." The player scooped up the ball and ran off.

Moving at a caterpillar's crawl, Martin slowly made it to his feet. His head throbbed. His chest felt like one big ache. Each breath hurt.

He had never been more embarrassed in his entire life. And that was the worst pain of all.

As soon as he was able, Martin packed up the camera, hefted the box, and limped off the field.

Marge was less than sympathetic. "If I had known you were going to be running out in front of trucks, I would never have let you take up photography in the first place."

"It was a football player," he corrected, "not a truck."

"Same thing." Marge fitted a butterfly bandage over the cut on his cheek with swift professional movements. Her touch was cool and reassuring. But not her tone. "I can't believe you just stood there and let him run over you."

"I was sort of busy," he said, and hoped the camera wasn't busted beyond all repair.

"All right." She fitted her hands around his side. "Take a deep breath."

He did so, working to keep his face calm.

"Did that hurt?"

"No," he fibbed.

"You seem okay. Bruised beyond belief, but

intact." She inspected his side, and Martin tried not to flinch. "Maybe I ought to have the doctor take a look at you anyway."

"I'm all right, Mom."

"All right, he says. With a shiner the size of my frying pan coming up on the side of his face." She lifted herself up to eye level. "Which is exactly what I will apply to your head if you try any such foolishness again."

"It wasn't foolishness," he said stubbornly.

Fire flashed in her dark eyes. "I've got too much on my mind right now to put up with nonsense from you, mister," she snapped. "You will stay out of the way of all football players and other flying objects, is that clear?"

Mr. Carruthers's response could not have been more different. "So you're becoming involved in your work. Good, that's very good."

"Maybe you should come talk to my mother," Martin said. "She doesn't think so."

"Mothers are not in my jurisdiction," Mr. Carruthers replied. "Good pictures are. You cannot take good pictures unless you are involved in your work. Becoming involved means taking risks. That is a fact of life, and applies to everything from photography to faith. Sometimes you just have to act on gut feeling, and place your logic to one side."

They were walking up towards the school's main entrance, Martin timing his steps to those of Mr. Carruthers. They had agreed to meet in front of the school when Martin had called the evening before and described his week. It was time, Mr. Carruthers had replied, to see the results of Martin's efforts.

Mr. Carruthers lifted his cane and rapped sharply on the door's metal frame. He waited a moment, then repeated the gesture. Just as he was about to do it a third time, the door flew open. Out popped the scowling face of the school's head custodian, a ferocious little man by the name of Jenkins. The entire school, teachers and principal included, lived in abject terror of the bestubbled janitor.

Martin took an involuntary step back.

But before Mr. Jenkins could open his mouth and take a bite from them, he recognized the old man. "Harry! What on earth brings you around here?"

"Hello, Jenks," Mr. Carruthers replied with a smile. "How have you been keeping?"

"Not bad, not bad, can't complain." Mr. Jenkins shifted the stump of his unlit stogie around so he could grin and expose discolored teeth. "Staying busy keeping all these folks in line. You know how it is."

"Sorry to bother you," Mr. Carruthers said, "but they made me give back my key when I retired."

"No bother, no bother at all," Mr. Jenkins replied. "Great to see you again. What can I do for you?"

"I was hoping to work in the darkroom a little," Mr. Carruthers replied, and motioned Martin forward. "I'd also like to introduce a new friend of mine. Jenks, meet Martin Powell."

"What say, Martin. What say."

"Nice to meet you, uh, Mr. Jenkins."

"Martin is showing quite a bit of promise," Mr.

Carruthers went on. "I'd like to ask if maybe you might manage to find him a key."

Martin could not disguise his amazement. A key to the school?

"If you vouch for him, don't see why not." Mr. Jenkins winked. "I might've forgot to hand in a key sometime back, you know?"

"I'd be most grateful," Mr. Carruthers said seriously.

Mr. Jenkins turned and inspected Martin with a keen eye. "What'd you do to your face, son?"

"I got hit by a football player."

"While taking photographs of their practice," Mr. Carruthers added hastily. "All in the line of duty."

"More like the line of fire, from the looks of things." Mr. Jenkins narrowed his eyes. "You're not gonna cause me any trouble now, are you?"

"Nosir."

"A polite kid. I like that. Not like a lot of those hanging around the halls these days." Mr. Jenkins nodded. "I suppose it's all right, then. Just you remember, though, you're to go straight to the darkroom and back out again, you hear?"

"No place else," Martin promised solemnly.

Mr. Jenkins pushed open the door. "You two go get started with your work. I'll see if I can find that key and bring it back to you."

"Much obliged, Jenks."

"Anytime, Harry. Anytime at all. And you remember what I said, kid. No trouble." Mr. Jenkins turned and shuffled off down the hall.

Developing the negatives was a laborious, time-consuming process. The Hasselblad film had to be unwound from its cartridges and fed into a larger developing spool. Mr. Carruthers made Martin change all the Graflex plates himself, saying practice made perfect. Then he stood at Martin's side, directing him through the series of chemical processes, showing him how to mark the time on the little blackboard screwed into the side wall. Always write it down, Mr. Carruthers said. Always. It saved the need to panic, and also the worry about losing valuable pictures when he began working on different things at once.

The negatives didn't look like much, after all that work. But Mr. Carruthers seemed satisfied with the results, so Martin didn't say anything. Once the film was dry, he showed Martin how to set the negatives out on the lighting tray and look at them through the loop, or magnifying glass. All the images were reversed in pigment, so that white was black and black white.

"This is worse than trying to focus upside down," Martin declared.

"Don't look at the image itself," Mr. Carruthers said. "Look at the focus. See how these lines are blurred? And look at the picture's layout. Look at this one—all the heads are chopped off; you had your camera angle too low. Later you will learn to set these aside and save yourself time. But for now we will develop pictures of everything, so you can study your results."

The atmosphere in the darkroom was very companionable. Work on the prints was done by a soft red development lamp, a light which would not affect black and white printing papers. The red was very rich and very dim, so that the corners of the tiny room were lost in shadows. It added to Martin's feeling of being initiated into secret mysteries.

The negatives were fitted onto the big machine at the back, then the long bellows were moved up and down until the image was in focus. Then the image machine's light was switched off, and a sheet of photographic paper was pulled from the box and set in place. The machine's timer was set at four seconds, then pushed in. A moment of waiting, then the bright white light came on, clicked like an egg timer, and at four seconds went out, leaving them both blinking in the dim red light.

Mr. Carruthers was a patient teacher. He explained over and over what he was doing, how he first placed the printing papers in the developer and then, after carefully watching the timer on the wall, transferred them to the fixer and then to the water bath. The smell from the chemicals was pungent, but not unpleasant. A little fan perched high up on one wall hummed cheerfully, pushing in fresh air. Martin found the whole process fascinating. Especially once Mr. Carruthers moved aside and began talking Martin through the development process himself.

The results, however, were disappointing in the extreme.

They began with the Graflex negatives, the camera used on the football practice field. Image after image was taken out and set into the machine and shot and developed. Every one of them was out of focus. Every single one.

After awhile Martin was able to tell from the negatives that the lines were not sharp enough. He worked the bellows up and down, saw how the images did not turn crisp, and said dejectedly, "We might as well just throw them all away."

"Nonsense," Mr. Carruthers replied, not in the least bothered by the results. "You need the practice at developing. Besides, you can oftentimes learn more from your errors than you can from your successes."

Each print was raised from the fixer and rinsed in water to take away all remaining chemicals, then clipped to the clothesline to dry. The pictures made a depressing line of mistakes. Most of them were so far out of focus that Martin could not even read the big numbers on the football jerseys.

Until the last picture.

Even as Martin worked the bellows, he knew this one was different. So did Mr. Carruthers. He crowded in behind Martin, and watched as the lines sharpened, and sharpened some more. The reversed image looked drawn with a precise pen.

Silently Mr. Carruthers gave Martin a sheet of printing paper. Martin found his hands were trembling slightly as he set the paper into place, adjusted the bellows a tiny notch, set the timer, and hit the switch. Four seconds and the light clicked off. Mr. Carruthers backed up a pace so Martin had room to slide the print into the development bath, watch the timer, watch, watch—

And see the picture he had been hoping for emerge into being. Sharp, crisp, perfect clarity.

He used the wooden tongs to lift the picture

from the developer bath and set it into the fixer. He watched the clock with only one eye, because he could not pull his attention away from the picture swimming below the liquid's surface. Finally he put it into the water bath.

Mr. Carruthers reached over his shoulder, plucked the picture from the water, hung it from an empty clothesline, and shone the developing light full force upon it. Then he took a step back.

They both looked at the picture in silence.

The tight end, the boy called Horner, appeared ready to leap from the picture and run into the room. His legs pumped so hard that even at the fast shutter speed, they held a slight blur. His upper body was twisted so that he looked back and over his left shoulder. His arms were raised high. His head was cocked up far enough for the sunlight to enter and illuminate the bottom half of his face, revealing a fierce grimace of concentration. The ball spun down and almost into his outstretched arms.

In the distance behind Horner, the line of scrimmage was a group of struggling bodies, all in perfect clarity. Over their heads stood the quarterback, his arm still extended from throwing the ball. The two boys, quarterback and end, were frozen in that moment of breathless connection, held together by the ball poised in midair.

Finally Mr. Carruthers asked quietly, "Was this the picture you took when you were hit?"

"Yes."

"A small price to pay," Mr. Carruthers said firmly. "Now tell me what you did differently here."

Martin explained about finding the book in the

case, and reading the passage about extending the field of focus by tightening the *f*-stop.

Mr. Carruthers listened in silence, his eyes never leaving the picture. "Where is the case?"

"I took it home," Martin replied, a little embarrassed by the feeling of possession he had over the equipment.

"Were all the filters and lenses still intact?"

"I guess so. At least all the little spaces were filled up."

"Excellent. I did not mention it for fear that it had all been lost." Mr. Carruthers nodded slowly. "Just as I said. You have great talent, my boy."

Martin glanced at the other clothesline, the one which held the long line of failures. "One picture out of thirty?"

Mr. Carruthers turned and fastened him with a somber gaze. "Listen to me, Martin. Photography is too important for me to joke about. I tell you with all sincerity, you have the three ingredients of greatness here. Do you know what they are?"

Martin shook his head.

"Very well, then. I will tell you. You have talent. How much, it is too early to tell, but talent is in truth the least important of the three, so long as it is there to some degree. The other two ingredients are drive and the willingness to take great pains. Without those two, talent means nothing. But you have spent hours practicing, you have read a book you found on your own, and you have applied what you have read." Mr. Carruthers turned back to the picture. "And now look at the result."

Martin did not know what to say.

"All right, back to work," Mr. Carruthers said, abruptly turning around. "You will find the frame for the Hasselblad negatives up there on the top shelf. Be a good lad and pull it down. Thank you."

The Hasselblad negatives were in a roll, like ordinary thirty-five-millimeter film, only broader. The holder for the larger Graflex negatives was set aside, the Hasselblad holder fitted with the negatives, and the developing process began once more.

They began working as a team, and the procedure went much faster. Martin turned the dial to the next negative, adjusted the bellows to bring the negative into focus, fitted in a photographic paper, and hit the switch. He then handed it to Mr. Carruthers, who worked the development baths. In less than an hour all the pictures were hung up and drying.

Mr. Carruthers pulled three pictures from the long line and hung them alongside the photograph of Dan Horner. They were the best of the shots of the apple islands rising in the dark shadow bowl, the tree limb growing sparkling jewel leaves, and the eyeglass shadow dripping tears.

Mr. Carruthers's silence was the highest praise Martin could ever have dreamed of receiving.

They stood and looked from one picture to another for a very long time. Finally Mr. Carruthers pointed to the tree limb and said, "This one is very good. You have shown a remarkable ability to use the power of light and shadow. But this—" He pointed to the eyeglasses. "This is a work of art."

"Thank you," Martin said softly.

"Would you tell me what is behind it?"

His eyes on the picture, Martin replied, "They were my father's glasses. He died last year."

When Mr. Carruthers did not reply, Martin risked a glance. The old man was nodding slowly, his eyes on the picture. "Would you mind a bit of advice?"

"Sure," Martin replied.

"It has nothing to do with making pictures," Mr. Carruthers said. "Well, perhaps that is not entirely true. I suppose you will have to decide that for yourself."

Martin waited, wondering where the old man was headed.

"Pain is a part of life," Mr. Carruthers said. "So is grief. So are the isolation and loneliness that pain and grief make us feel."

For some reason, Martin felt as though some barrier within himself was being stripped away. Part of him wanted to run away and hide what the old man was able to see without even looking his way. But he could not. He felt glued to the spot.

Mr. Carruthers kept his eyes on the picture. "A good artist uses everything life presents to him in the creation of his art. But the question, my young friend, is whether it is applied in a positive or negative direction. Do you understand what I am saying?"

"I—" Martin swallowed and tried again. "I'm not sure."

"Some people take their anger and their pain and they hold on to it for all their life. It is the only thing they have to fill the emptiness within themselves. That is a negative direction, and it leads to negative art. Other people seek a source of goodness and hope and love and light. When they are presented with pain or sorrow, they balance the bad with the good. In the dark times, they struggle to return to the light. They hold to the rock, and their art reflects both this struggle and this direction."

Mr. Carruthers turned to look upon Martin's face. "This, my friend, is positive art. But the secret to positive art is that it cannot be done alone. A person who moves alone will inevitably move into the darkness. No one moving alone through life is strong enough to avoid the false paths. So if you want to take what life gives you and give it a positive meaning, a positive direction, then you must have the help of God."

Martin's football picture was given a full third of the school newspaper's front page. The headline above it shouted, FOOTBALL SEASON OPENS SATURDAY! The caption beneath the picture read, "Tight end Dan Horner and quarterback Kevin Murphy practice their touchdown-making skills in preparation for Saturday's big game against Eastwood High. Photo: Martin Powell."

Martin walked on air all day long.

After classes Monday he stopped by the cramped cubicles used by both the newspaper and the school yearbook staffs. He found Janice banging away on a battered typewriter and chewing on the end of a mangled pencil. She looked up as he swung into view and proclaimed, "High-class journalism it ain't. But it's a living."

"I got a picture on the front page," Martin declared, saying it just to hear how it sounded.

"Yeah, I saw." Janice inspected him with a

jaundiced air. "Don't worry, you'll get used to it."

"I was thinking maybe I should find out what's going on," Martin said. "You know, what's coming up that you'll want me to take pictures of around school. Other than the games, of course, which I already know about."

Every typewriter up and down the cluttered room was suddenly silent. Janice's jaw dropped three inches, then she shut it with a click. "You want to run that by me one more time?"

"You know," Martin said. "Sort of set up a schedule or something."

Heads popped out of neighboring cubicles. A shaggy-haired boy wearing a T-shirt that almost reached his knees came over and asked Janice, "Am I really hearing this?"

"How can I be dreaming if I'm not asleep?" Janice asked him back. "Am I asleep?"

"No more than usual." The boy turned to Martin. "You Powell?"

"Yes."

He stuck out an ink-stained hand. "Bob Flickinger. My friends call me Flick. I'm as much in charge of the yearbook as anybody is."

"What do your enemies call you?" Janice said, and then explained to Martin, "Don't pay Flick any attention. He's like a bark that lost the dog. You want anything done around here, come see me."

"Thanks, I—"

"All right," a voice growled, as the outer door slammed. "Why don't I hear any work getting done?"

Two pairs of eyes rolled towards the ceiling. The

heads which had poked out from their cubicles disappeared like turtles retreating into their shells. Janice whispered a soft, "Sarge."

A heavyset woman with bulldog features set in a permanent scowl thumped into view. "Loafing again. I knew it. Every time I turn around you start treating this place like a country club."

"That's not true, Miss Spurles," Flick replied, his voice almost singing the words.

"Nobody's irreplaceable, Mr. Flickinger." She stomped up close and thrust her face up close to Flick. In one hand she grasped a long solid-wood ruler whose edges were scarred and chipped. She kneaded it constantly, as though barely able to resist the urge to apply it to the side of some poor student's head. "Haven't I told you that before?"

"Only about a hundred thousand times, Miss Spurles," Flick half-said, half-sang.

"Don't you get smart with me, Mister," she snapped. Then she whirled around to face Martin. "Who's this? Haven't I told you that visitors are strictly forbidden?"

Martin found himself trying to climb the cubicle wall behind him. Backwards.

"This is Martin Powell, Miss Spurles," Janice replied for him. "The photographer."

She shoved one of the ugliest faces Martin had ever seen within inches of his nose. "Didn't you take that picture in the newspaper?"

Martin yammered, "Y-y-yes, Ma'am."

"Hmph." She backed up enough for him to feel safe enough to breathe. "Are you going to be as much trouble as those two other so-called photographers?"

"Martin was just saying," Janice replied, "how he'd like to set up a schedule of events that we want pictures of."

"He did, did he?" Steel-gray eyes inspected every pore on Martin's face. "Well, don't just stand around blabbering. Give it to him!"

"We were just going to, Miss Spurles," Flick replied in his overly cheerful singsong.

"All of you get back to work! You've been given a great privilege, being allowed to stay here after hours." Miss Spurles wheeled about and stomped towards the door. Two mouths silently parodied her words as she went on, "And with privilege comes responsibility!"

The door slammed closed, and the entire room heaved a great sigh of relief. Martin released his grip on the cubicle wall and asked shakily, "Who was that?"

"The Sarge," Janice replied.

"The nemesis of my daily existence," Flick said.

"Sarge is the teacher responsible for the yearbook," Janice explained.

"She's responsible for my daily headaches," Flick said. "She's responsible for giving me ulcers and a bad heart."

"You could always quit," Janice offered.

"What, and give up all this privilege?" Flick motioned with his head. "Come on, Powell, let's get you that list before you change your mind."

From the newspaper offices Martin walked downstairs to the Industrial Arts hall. He walked back through the machine room and saw that the darkroom door was ajar. He approached with a grin and said, "I was wondering if you two had vanished from the face of the earth."

Floyd pushed the door farther open. He was dressed as before in head-to-toe black. "Well, well, well. If it isn't our hot-shot peon."

Martin stopped in the doorway and felt his grin slip from his face. "What's the matter?"

"Nothing's the matter, Peon," Floyd said. Behind him Ellen stayed busy with some task. She did not look up, did not say a word. As far as she was concerned, he might as well not have been there. Floyd said, "Didn't you see we were getting low on supplies?"

"Sure, but I—"

"Did I or did I not tell you that it was your responsibility to deal with the Cro-Magnon Coach?"

Martin found himself growing angry without understanding why. "You told me."

"So do it." Floyd thrust a paper at him. "Be sure you get everything I've noted here, especially the color film."

"Right," Martin said, and started off.

"Hey, Peon," Floyd called out. Reluctantly Martin turned around. Floyd went on, "Getting lucky one time doesn't change a thing."

"What are you talking about?"

Floyd smirked. "You just remember who's king."

Martin bit back his reply and turned away. Suddenly he wanted to be anywhere but there. "I'll go talk to the coach."

The coach was busy berating a player as Martin approached. Martin stopped out of range and watched as the cowed player grew steadily smaller under the coach's roar. The coach finally slapped the side of the player's helmet and sent him scooting back out onto the playing field. His face was red from the effort of all that yelling, which made him look even meaner than usual.

Coach Lynch blew a long blast on his whistle and shouted, "What is that you're playing out there? Football? You think that's football?" He shook his head in disgust. "You girls want to play Eastwood on Saturday, you'd better do better than that! You don't, and I'm not gonna even leave a greasy stain!"

Martin started backing away.

The movement caught Coach Lynch's eye. "Hey, Powell! Yeah, you." He motioned him over.

"I can come back later," Martin said. "Maybe now's not such a good time."

"Get over here, Powell!" Lynch ordered.

Reluctantly Martin walked forward, ready to turn and flee at the first sign of trouble.

Coach Lynch leaned over and inspected him, his permanent scowl looking even more ferocious at such close quarters. "That's some shiner you got coming up there."

One player detached himself from the scrimmage and came trotting over. He unfastened his helmet, and Martin realized it was Dan Horner. Martin's stomach twinged. He wasn't up to having both of them on him at once.

But Horner grinned and said, "Hey, get a look at your kisser. Did I do that?"

"Who told you to come over here?" Coach

Lynch barked. "Back on the field, Horner."

"Sure, Coach," Horner replied, still grinning. "I just wanted to say thanks to the nerd here for the great shot."

"His name is Powell!" Lynch bellowed. "Martin Powell. Use it."

"Right. Anyway, thanks. It was great." And with that he turned and trotted back into the line.

Coach Lynch kept his eye on Martin. "You had a doctor take at look at that, son?"

"My mother did. She's a nurse."

"I guess that's all right, then. Injuries have to be taken care of, otherwise they can cause you trouble." Two stubby fingers felt the skin around the outside of his eye with surprising gentleness. "That hurt?"

"No," Martin lied.

"I guess you'll live. You going to cover the game on Saturday?"

"Yessir."

The scowl deepened, and Martin realized with a shock that the coach was smiling. "Guess maybe we better fit you with a helmet, if you keep coming in close for those shots."

Confused by the man's unexpected friendliness, Martin held up the paper in his hand. "This is for you."

"What's that you got here?"

"We need some things for the darkroom."

Swiftly Coach Lynch scanned the page, then handed it back. "Looks okay. Requisition forms are on my desk. Take one, fill it out, leave it for me to sign."

Martin accepted the sheet with numb fingers.

"Thanks," he said feebly.

"Don't mention it. Good picture, by the way. Nice to work with somebody who knows his business." The coach turned and stomped away, blowing fiercely on his whistle as he went.

The camera store to which Mr. Carruthers took him was unimpressive in the extreme. The store was downtown, an area where Martin almost never went. It had wire-mesh fences over the two windows and dusty old displays. Instead of the vast array of equipment found in shopping center stores, one window held only five cameras. Martin stopped to look at them. The cameras looked old-fashioned and clumsy—Leitz, Yashima, a couple of Hasselblads, and the biggest Nikon he had ever seen. The prices were unbelievable. The other window held three shelves of used equipment, and even they were more expensive than the new stuff in the shopping mall stores. Over the door was written in faded gilt, JOSEPH SINGER, CAMERAS AND PHOTOGRAPHIC SUPPLIES.

Martin asked Mr. Carruthers, "Why are we here?"

Mr. Carruthers smiled and replied, "Ask me that in a year's time."

He pushed open the old-fashioned door, which rang a bell in an unseen back room. They entered a narrow shop that smelled musty. Light filtering through the dirty front windows was caught by dust motes hanging in the air. Two waist-high cases with glass tops ran the length of the room, with a narrow space in the middle for customers.

A cranky voice called out, "Hold your horses, I'm coming. I'm coming."

"Take your time, Joseph," Mr. Carruthers replied, glancing casually around the room.

"Harry? Is that you?" A dusty curtain whipped back to reveal a shrunken gnome with a nasty expression. He squinted through wire-rimmed spectacles and declared, "I thought they told me you were dead."

"Not yet," Mr. Carruthers replied. "Joseph, I'd like—"

"I'm sure they told me that," the gnome said, and stumped forward. He reached across the glass-topped counter and poked Mr. Carruthers in the arm. "Hmph. Guess it's you, after all."

"You don't have to seem so disappointed," Mr. Carruthers replied crossly.

"Don't like saying good-bye to friends," the gnome snapped. "Like it even less when I have to do it twice."

"Well, I guess I like this," Mr. Carruthers said. "I come by to pay my respects to an old buddy, and he gets upset because I'm not dead."

The outer door pushed open, and the unseen bell clanged once more. "Joseph, I need—" The tall dark-haired man caught sight of Mr. Carruthers, and his eyes widened. "Harry! Good grief, man, I heard you were—"

"Don't say it," Mr. Carruthers snapped. "Retired for two years and everybody on earth starts trying to put me in a box."

"Not me, man," the tall man protested. "I'm tickled pink to see you. How've you been?"

"Quite well, thank you," Mr. Carruthers replied crisply. "All rumors to the contrary."

"Hey, that's great." The man turned around and said, "Joseph, I got a major shoot coming up this afternoon. I need some of those portable—"

"Listen to the big shot," the gnome scoffed. "Gets his name in the magazines, thinks he's somebody special, starts barging into my shop, pushing my old friends aside, wants to be first."

The tall man turned sheepish. "Look, it's nothing like that. I've just been rushing around like crazy this morning, trying to get everything set up. The agency's sending me a model down from New York and I've still got a ton of work left to do."

"Ah, now he pulls out the excuses," the gnarled little man snorted. "Wait a little and he'll be telling us his grandmother's died. For the thirty-second time."

"Martin, this is Frank Simpson," Mr. Carruthers said, still too peeved to look at the tall man directly. "Frank specializes in commercial work and fashion photography."

"Specializes in silliness, you mean," Joseph corrected, looking directly at Martin for the first time. "He takes these skinny women, dresses them up in too much makeup, drapes them over cars and trees and bridges and what-not, and tells them to look like they want to kiss the camera."

Frank Simpson grinned and shrugged heavy shoulders. "It's a living."

"It's silliness," Joseph countered. "Such a talent going to waste."

Frank Simpson was not the least put off by the little man's criticism. He stuck out his hand and said to Martin, "Nice to meet you, kid. You a photographer?"

"Yes," Mr. Carruthers answered for him, still looking off into the distance.

"Aw, hey, Harry, don't get your hair up," Frank soothed, winking at Martin. "I felt real bad about missing your funeral, and now look, I get a second chance. Ain't that great?"

"Joseph," Mr. Carruthers said, "do you still have that gun underneath the cash register?"

"Maybe I should come back later," Frank Simpson said.

"You stay right where you are," Joseph ordered. He then said to Mr. Carruthers, "Harry, I am too old to take care of any more of your students."

"He's not one of my students," Mr. Carruthers replied. "I'm retired, remember? And by the sound of things, I've already got one foot in the grave, so I need somebody to take him on when I'm gone."

"I don't know, Harry," Frank Simpson said, winking a second time at Martin. "You look pretty good to me for an old crank. Got at least a couple more months on the old clock."

"If I had any sense I'd close up this firetrap and retire too," Joseph said, ignoring Frank Simpson. "I barely have the energy to look after the clients I've got."

With precise motions Mr. Carruthers opened the manila folder he held under his arm and laid three photographs on the counter face down. "Turn these over and tell me that again," he replied.

Joseph hesitated. "Three pictures," he muttered. "What am I supposed to tell from just three pictures?"

Frank Simpson walked around the counter to stand beside Joseph. He towered over the little man. "Turn them over, Joseph. If you don't, I will."

"Keep your hands off the merchandise," Joseph snapped, not moving. "And get back on the other side of the counter where you belong."

Frank did not move.

"Why just three pictures, Harry?" Joseph demanded.

"Because this remarkable young man has only been taking pictures," Mr. Carruthers replied, "for one month."

Joseph fastened Martin with a beady gaze. "Is that true?"

"I messed around with my dad's camera some," Martin replied. "But I guess I've really just started."

"Hmph." Joseph returned his gaze to the three blank sheets. "Then it's far too early to tell anything."

"Turn them over, Joseph," Mr. Carruthers said quietly.

The little gnome of a man gave an exasperated snort, then reached out one hand. His knuckles were knotted and swollen with arthritis. He scrabbled a moment, trying to grasp the edge. Then he flipped over the first picture. It was the shadow tree with water leaves. Frank Simpson bent closer, his eyes narrowing in concentration. Joseph slapped his shoulder. Frank backed off a fraction of an inch, his attention not slipping from the picture.

Another photograph was turned over, this one of the football players. Frank gave a little grunt and moved closer once more. This time Joseph did not complain. The third picture was turned over, the one of the crying spectacles. The room was so still Martin could hear the footsteps of pedestrians walking down the sidewalk outside the store.

The silence held for a long moment, then Joseph said quietly, "What was it you needed, Frank?"

"Two more klieg lights," Frank said, lowering his head even closer to the counter. His forehead was knotted in concentration. "We're doing an outside shoot tonight."

"You know where they are," Joseph said, his face still turned towards the pictures.

"Sure, thanks." Frank did not move.

"I suppose you'll be wanting frames for these," Joseph said.

"If it's not too much trouble," Mr. Carruthers said, all politeness now. "And a neutral *passe- partout*, please."

Joseph finally looked up. "You're going to have him do color also?"

"These days, a guy doesn't have much choice," Frank Simpson replied for Mr. Carruthers. The tall man raised his head and looked at Martin. "What were you using, kid?"

Martin found it difficult to keep his voice steady as he said, "A Hasselblad for the shadow prints. And a Graflex for the action picture."

Frank Simpson grinned at Mr. Carruthers. "Still making them start off with those old clunkers, Harry?"

"They served you well enough," Mr. Carruthers replied quietly.

"Yeah, guess so." The tall man glanced at his watch and bolted upright. "Gotta move. Listen, kid, Harry knows where my studio is. If you like, stop by and I'll show you around sometime."

"That'd be great, thanks."

"You'll do no such thing," Joseph snapped. "You'll learn nothing but nonsense from this big galoot."

Frank smiled at Martin. "Give me a call," he said, before slipping through the back curtain and clattering down unseen stairs.

"Come back tomorrow," Joseph said to Martin. "I'll have them ready."

Martin hesitated, then asked, "How much—"

"Thanks a lot, Joseph," Mr. Carruthers interrupted, and motioned with his cane at the door. "You won't be disappointed."

"After three o'clock," Joseph said crossly. "I'm an old man. I don't move so fast these days."

"He'll be by after school," Mr. Carruthers assured him. "Take care."

Martin waited until the next evening to announce to his mother, "I've got a job."

She dropped the spoon she was using to stir the soup. "What?"

"In a camera store," he went on. "Downtown."

"What do you need money for?"

"I get paid in equipment," he explained. "It's only when I have the time. Saturday mornings, maybe a couple of afternoons a week. Mr. Carruthers arranged it. He says I'll learn a lot working there. I can take a bus."

Marge started stirring the soup again. "Don't you think you're taking this photography thing a little too fast?"

Instead of replying, he drew the three framed prints from their wrapping paper. "Look."

The pictures were set in white metal frames. Inside was an off-white *passe-partout*, which Martin now knew meant a sort of second cardboard frame under the glass. The cardboard frame was a full four inches wide. The photographs themselves were printed on paper eight inches high and ten inches broad, and with this cream-colored paper border, the frames were almost twice as big as the pictures themselves. When Martin had gone in to pick up the photographs, Mr. Singer had explained that they used these secondary frames to amplify the picture's power. The frame within a frame acted as a sort of magnet for the eye, drawing the viewer closer.

His mother sort of half-turned around, still involved with her cooking. But that first glance was enough to hold her. She tapped the ladle on the side of the pan, set it down, wiped her hands, and faced him. She started to reach for the picture, then stopped. "You took that?"

"In our backyard." It was the picture of the shadow branch.

"It's very nice," she said quietly. "I had no idea—" she started, then changed her mind. "Show me the others."

The next one was of the football players. Somehow the framing had made the picture come even more alive. Marge's eyes widened.

He waited a moment, then lifted the third picture.

In a swift reflexive motion, his mother crossed her arms in front of her chest. She backed up a half-step and was stopped by the stove. She opened her mouth, then closed it. She tried again. Her voice was unsteady as she said, "Hang them in your room."

Martin dropped the picture onto his lap. "What?"

"Use a wall in your own room," she said, and Martin realized she was shaking. "I don't want to have to . . ." Then she turned and walked from the kitchen.

Martin stared at the empty space where his mother had stood. Somehow he felt happy and sad and empty and excited all at the same time.

The football game on Saturday was very different from practice. Totally different.

Friday afternoon the school held its first pep rally. Martin had used his brand-new special pass to get out of class a half hour early and prepare his equipment. The rally had taken place in the school gym. Martin had a great time being down on the floor, taking pictures of the players as they sat grinning self-consciously, shooting photographs of the school president and the principal and the team captain and the cheerleaders, until he spotted Floyd and Ellen.

A group of older students lounged up at the top of the bleachers. The only reason Martin noticed them at all was because the school president looked right at them when he said that those who didn't enjoy rallies and school sports should not spoil it for the others. The group had replied with a loud raspberry. Martin had looked up, and spotted Floyd and Ellen right there in the middle of them. They were dressed as always in black, and appeared extremely bored with the whole deal. But even from that distance he could tell that their eyes were on him. And something about the way they looked at him took a lot of the fun out of the rally.

The memory of their look stayed with him right up to game time. He walked through the jostling crowds that Saturday evening, for some reason half-afraid he would spot them. Instead he found Janice, the writer for the school paper.

"Well, well, if it isn't the hotshot shooter," she smirked. "Ready to capture our gallant boys in action?"

He nodded. "Have you seen Floyd or Ellen?"

"Are you kidding? They made it to the two final games last year, and only because Coach Lynch threatened to close the darkroom if they didn't."

Martin relaxed. "Where should I leave my stuff?"

"I guess over there by the players' bench." She looked at him. "Are you having trouble with the terrible twins?"

"I don't know," he replied honestly. "I hope not."

A shout rose from the crowd as the teams trotted onto the field. Janice gave his shoulder a playful punch. "I'm up in the stands with some of the gang. Come see us if you take a break."

The gang. Said as though he were a member too. "Are there always so many people here for a high school football game?"

"Some people are saying we've got a chance to make the state finals," Janice replied, her casual tone at odds with the excitement in her eyes. "If you follow that sort of thing."

"Which you don't," Martin said. "You're just here to do a job, right?"

"You got it." She turned and started climbing the bleachers. "See ya."

"Bye." Martin lugged his case over behind the bench. When the players broke from their huddle a couple glanced his way, but nobody said anything.

The noise was loud and came from both sides of the field. The visiting team had brought a very large cheering section of their own. Two bands, one from each school, competed for attention. The players threw blocks on each other and shouted and slapped high fives and ran pass patterns and jammed fists onto one another's shoulder pads.

Martin ran through a final check of his own, and felt his adrenaline soar into high gear.

The September evening was long and warm, but already the big field lights were turned on. Martin was shooting the big Graflex with a flash for only the second time—the first time was at the pep rally the day before. Flash was easier in one respect, because it meant he didn't have to fiddle with the light meter. And he could avoid shadows getting in his way, because the flash came from the same direction as the camera.

But it was also another new thing to worry about.

The nicest thing about the flash was how it looked. It had a chrome-plated barrel the size of a flashlight—for the four heavy-duty batteries—attached to a shallow chrome bowl that was broader than his hand.

It dressed the camera up like crazy.

Each flash required a different bulb. Martin laid a box of the big bulbs out beside the film plates. He fitted one bulb into the flash, slid in the negative plate, pulled out the protective sleeve, and hefted the camera just as the coin was tossed. He was ready.

Two hours later, halfway through the fourth quarter, the score was still tied at seven all.

Both of the teams had fought a bitter struggle. Five yards given here, two there, but neither had been able to break through their opponents' defense since scoring in the game's early minutes. The field was churned into mud. The crowd had shouted itself hoarse, Martin included.

He had shot all but two negatives. Those he was holding just in case Westover scored. He was terrifically disappointed with his work. He had made a lot of mistakes.

Four times he had gotten so carried away with the game he had forgotten to take out the protective sleeve, and missed shots. Twice he had forgotten to turn the negative over after shots and had taken new pictures, double-exposing the negatives. One of them was his only picture of their only touchdown. He would be lucky if one shot would be usable.

Then came his break.

With less than three minutes left on the clock, Kevin Murphy worked a drive that pushed them over the fifty-yard line for the first time in the second half. He kept the ball himself and ran seven hard-driving plays in a row. The crowd screamed its approval. The cheerleaders leapt and danced, the band blazed and swiveled the big horns, the loudspeakers blared, the referee's whistle blew the two-minute warning.

Coach Lynch signaled for his last time-out. The referee blew his whistle once more. Kevin came trotting over. For some reason, Martin decided to follow.

The strain of the last seven plays was clearly evident on the quarterback's features. His dark hair was matted to his skull with sweat. His cheeks looked sunken in the stark overhead lighting. He took a swallow from the squeeze bottle, then let his arm hang limp at his side. His mouth hung open, and his chest heaved with the exertion of breathing. Coach Lynch settled one heavy arm on Kevin's shoulders. The coach had to lean over and shout in the player's ear to be heard, the crowd and the band were so loud.

Martin moved up closer.

The coach pointed out at the field and shouted something more. Kevin looked out, squinting as he tried to push aside his fatigue and concentrate on what the coach was saying. Martin raised his camera and focused. Behind the coach and player was the scoreboard with the lights showing the fourth quarter and tied score and less than two minutes on the clock.

Martin hit the trigger.

The coach dropped his arm and patted Kevin on the back, pushing him back out onto the field. Martin joined the rest of the crowd in urging the team on.

The team joined for a huddle. Kevin hesitated, looked back at the coach, who jabbed his finger downfield. Kevin bent over. The players clapped their hands and broke. Kevin took his position behind the center. He surveyed the lineup, bent over, made his call. The ball was snapped. Kevin backed up and searched.

Martin raised his camera, then froze just as he was hitting the trigger. In his excitement he had forgotten to turn the negative plate over. Again.

Kevin fired a bullet pass right into Dan Horner's open arms. The crowd went berserk. An opponent flew up and rammed into Dan, pushing him out of bounds at the twenty-two-yard line.

It was all over while Martin was still fumbling with the negative. He let the camera fall to his side. He had missed the game's biggest play.

The team's field-goal kicker ran out onto the field. Martin scampered around to the end-zone, and snapped a shot of the ball clearing the goalposts. But he knew it wasn't going to work out. The teams were so far away they would look like just a group of guys. The ball would be a little blurred speck at the top of the photo. Still, he took it just so he wouldn't miss that play as well.

While the crowd hooted and yelled its joy, and while Kevin was lifted onto the shoulders of his teammates, Martin packed up his camera and made his dejected way home.

But things didn't turn out as badly as Martin feared.

The photograph that he delivered to the newspaper showed the coach talking with Kevin on the sidelines. The scoreboard was slightly out of focus, but still perfectly readable. Coach Lynch looked ferocious. Murphy looked exhausted but determined. It was a good picture.

Even Janice unwound from her customary cynicism to compliment him, as much as she was able. What she actually said was, "The pair look almost human."

"Thanks," Martin replied, "a lot."

"But five gets you ten," she went on, "you're going to hear from the Snow Queen about it."

"Who?" By then it was clear to Martin that Janice was basically responsible for putting out the newspaper single-handedly. The others came and went like the wind, dropping off articles when and if it suited them. Miss Paisley stopped by from time to time, fanned the air and nervously patted her hair, refused to finish a sentence, and left.

"The Snow Queen," Janice repeated. "Nancy Starling. Otherwise known as the head cheerleader, school sweetheart, and girl voted most likely to live happily ever after."

"Also Kevin's girlfriend," Flick said, moving up behind them. "Not bad. I want that one for the yearbook."

"Get in line," Janice said smugly. "I've already got first dibs on it. Right, buddy?"

Martin looked at her. "Buddy?"

"I've got a great caption," Flick said. "Coach Lynch tells Murphy he should take the funny-shaped ball down to the other end of the field. Murphy becomes tired from the need to concentrate."

Janice dug an elbow into Flick's ribs. "Kevin is not dumb. Except when it comes to choosing his female company."

"Ah," Flick said with his habitual smirk. "You fail to understand the finer points of this matter."

"Such as?" Janice demanded.

"That Nancy Starling happens to be an absolute world-class beauty."

"There is more to life than looks," Janice said. "I think that's why I like this picture."

Martin looked at her. "What do you mean?"

"You make him look real." Janice shrugged. "I don't know how to explain it better than that."

Martin was still puzzling over that two days later when the paper came out. It was the second time that his name had been attached to a front-page picture, and now a lot of the school had seen him scrambling around the gym floor at the rally or running up and down the sidelines at the game. He was becoming a familiar face. Students he did not know said hello as he passed. Martin walked down the hall of the school, and for the first time felt as though he belonged.

He had just finished dialing out his locker's combination when a girl's voice behind him said, "Martin? Can I talk to you for a minute?"

He turned around and faced a vision. That was how he remembered it afterwards. A vision.

Nancy Starling had blond hair just one shade off of true white. Her eyebrows were startlingly pale, offset by the eyeliner and eye shadow which had been applied with an expert hand. Her figure was something to dream about. She flashed a brilliant smile. "I saw your picture of Kevin in the newspaper? The one of him with Coach Lynch?"

The little lilt she gave to the end of each sentence was as cute as everything else about her. Martin felt like he could dive into her blue eyes, they were so big. "Yes," he managed.

"It was really nice, I guess, but you know, Kevin worked so hard out there on the field, and he did so much, and I was just wondering, couldn't you have found a better picture than that?"

Martin was just about to surrender to her dulcet tones, and confess to having botched almost every other picture of the game, when a voice behind them said, "There you are. Where've you been?"

Kevin walked up and slipped his arm around Nancy's shoulders. Even Martin had to admit that it fitted there like hand and glove. They were made for each other. Big football star with the shoulders of an ox, dark features, and a jaw that looked made for Hollywood, and the blond-haired, blue-eyed cheerleader. Martin felt his hopes evaporate in a puff of defeat.

Kevin looked down at him from lofty heights. "You're that photographer. Powell, right?"

Martin nodded.

"Great picture of me and the coach."

Nancy Starling turned immensely peevish. "Kevin, why did you have to say that?"

"Because it was," he replied, totally confused. "Come on, we'll be late for class." He gave Martin an affable nod and steered her away. "Nice meeting you, kid. Keep up the good work."

Martin watched them move away, sighed, wondered why it was that they should wind up with everything, even happiness. He turned back to his locker.

He pulled open the door and found that somebody had slipped a note through the metal slats. He opened it, and felt his world stop cold.

Marty,
　We have decided your services as peon are no longer required. Drop off your darkroom key today. Sorry and all that.

　　　　　　　　　　Floyd

Martin was frantic by the time he arrived at Mr. Carruthers's house that afternoon. But the teacher's reaction startled him almost as much as the note from Floyd. The old man heard him out, then settled back in silence. Martin was baffled by this calm.

Finally Mr. Carruthers said quietly, "I'm not sure you should do anything."

"What?" Martin half-rose from his chair. "But they're kicking me out!"

"I realize that," the old man replied. "And according to the way the club is structured, they have every right to do so."

"But you don't understand! I want—"

"I understand perfectly," Mr. Carruthers interrupted, not raising his voice. "I understand that sometimes it is best to wait, hard as it may be."

Martin felt like tearing out his hair. "Wait for what?"

"Today is Tuesday," Mr. Carruthers said. "Why don't we give it until Monday and see what happens? In the meantime, keep yourself busy and try not to worry."

The first part of his instructions was easier to carry out than the second. Martin spent every free moment at Mr. Singer's shop, dusting off the counters, cleaning the windows, sorting through the cluttered back room, watching the little man deal with clients, meeting a number of his cronies.

But nothing could keep him from worrying.

His mother noticed that he was not eating, and asked him what was wrong. But he couldn't explain. To talk about it would mean trying to say why he wasn't doing anything, and he couldn't do that, because he didn't understand.

To make it worse, Mr. Carruthers had been taken ill and was in bed. When Martin went by on Thursday, Mrs. Carruthers said he would be indisposed for the rest of the week. So there was no chance of a reprieve. Martin slumped his way through school, avoided going anywhere near his old haunts, kept hold of the darkroom key as a last vestige of hope, and worried.

Friday morning Janice caught up with him in the halls. "You haven't been around the office this week. Anything the matter?"

Glumly Martin told her the news.

Janice was outraged. "They can't do that!"

"They can and they did," Martin replied.

"We'll see about that," she snapped, and stormed off.

During his second class of the day, a very flustered

Miss Paisley stuck her head in the door and said, "Oh, excuse me, but, well, might I please have a word with Martin Powell? That is, if it's not. . . ."

When Martin joined her in the hallway and the door was closed, Miss Paisley said, "Is it true what Janice has told me?"

"I've been sacked," Martin confirmed. "Kicked out of the photography club."

"But why?"

"They didn't say," Martin replied.

"Well, I don't know." Miss Paisley reached up to pat her wayward hair. "I thought you were such a nice young man, I mean, are a nice young man, of course. Why anyone would. . . . Oh dear, I do hate problems like this."

"So do I," Martin said, crestfallen.

"Yes, of course you do." A glint of resolve surfaced in Miss Paisley's eyes. "Well, I think your work has just been wonderful. And the newspaper certainly needs you. I intend to do something about this." With that she turned and walked away.

Miss Spurles sent a student to fetch him from his math class. When he knocked on her door, she left her class, stormed outside, slammed the door behind her, and demanded, "I want to know the meaning of this nonsense."

"I don't know," Martin replied.

"Somebody has stepped out of bounds," Miss Spurles snapped, her chin jutting out at a dangerous angle, "and is about to receive a piece of my mind. Back to your class, mister." She stomped back into her room and slammed the door shut behind her.

Martin stood there for a moment and knew a brief sense of satisfaction. At least they wouldn't get away without having their feathers singed.

At lunch a trio of football players led by Dan Horner approached his table. "Hey, kid, is it true what we heard about you getting the boot?"

Martin nodded. "I'm history."

"Says who, the black knight and his sidekick?" Dan Horner looked mad enough to turn the table into matchsticks. "Leave this with us, kid."

"Wait 'til the coach hears about it," one of his buddies agreed.

Martin watched them walk away, and knew the first flicker of hope.

But he heard nothing more before school let out for the weekend, and by the time he arrived downtown at Mr. Singer's shop, the dark clouds had settled in once again.

Mr. Singer noticed and asked him what was the matter. When Martin explained, the old man snorted and said, "So? And they took away your chance to take pictures as well? Your talent?"

"But it's the school club," Martin complained. "The darkroom and the newspaper and everything."

"No, not everything." The gnarled little man reached across the counter and punched Martin with a knobby finger. "You are still you, yes?"

"I guess so."

"No, no guesses. Photographers do not make good pictures with guesses. You must know. Listen, young man, and I will tell you a secret. Life for an artist is not always Easy Street. There. You have just been given a valuable lesson that took me years to learn." Mr. Singer made brushing motions towards the door. "Go. Take that box of supplies over to Frank Simpson's studio. And lose your long face somewhere on the way. Long faces we do not need around this shop."

Frank Simpson's studio was in an old warehouse at the border of the dingy section of town. It was a twenty-minute walk from the store, and Martin was sweating hard by the time he arrived.

Frank opened the door himself, and cried, "Just who I was looking for! Get in here, quick."

Martin followed him up the broad stone stairs and into a vast chamber that occupied one entire floor of the warehouse. The ceilings were a full twenty feet high. The brick walls were whitewashed. The floors were polished wood. A darkroom was built into one far corner. Two stages were set up at opposite ends of the room, one with a pale ivory background, the other strung with richly colored drapes.

Frank led him to the middle of the room where a small computer was set upon a crystal stand. "Just dump that stuff anywhere. My assistant's sick, and I've been going crazy trying to adjust these lights by myself." When Martin had set down the supplies and joined him, Frank pointed to the overhanging lights. "We've got to set them so there won't be any shadows, and also no light reflecting through the stand onto the camera."

"Tricky," Martin guessed.

"You said it. Okay, move that one a little to the left. No, too far. Back, back, stop. All right, move over to that one. Can you shift the screen . . . yeah, that's it." Frank bent and focused the camera resting on the tall tripod. From his crouched position he muttered, "Why a crystal stand, I ask. Why not something easy, like dropping me and the computer from an airplane at thirty thousand feet. No, no, these advertising guys, they get an idea for a gimmick, and it's got to be just so."

Frank straightened, and noticed Martin's expression. "What's the matter with you?"

Martin moved from light to light, explaining what had happened as he went.

"Okay, that's great. Now the next one." Frank resumed his stooped posture. "What did Harry tell you?"

"Mr. Carruthers? He said for me to wait."

Frank Simpson did not disagree. "I used to fight like the dickens against a lot of what Harry laid on me. But it's amazing how often the old guy is right."

"I don't see how," Martin said dejectedly. "Not this time."

"Yeah, that sounds a lot like me." Frank smiled. "Almost exactly what I told him when he started laying his ideas about faith on me, as a matter of fact. I couldn't see how photography had anything to do with religion. Know what he said?"

"I can imagine."

"Yeah, I'll bet. Okay, slide up on that ladder and pull the top light over a notch. Great. Yeah, Harry said there was a world of difference between religion and faith. He was talking about developing a personal relationship with Jesus, not doing something for the outside world. Being the rebel that I was, I laughed in his face."

"What did Mr. Carruthers say?"

"Nothing much. He never got bothered about what I said. I guess he felt like his job was to share his faith with me. After that I was pretty much free to do with it what I wanted. I guess that's the only reason I ever listened to him in the first place."

Frank held up his hand. "Okay, hold it right there. I think we've finally got it."

He took several quick pictures, refocused and shot again. "That ought to do the trick. Now let's see if we can use those spots to our advantage, do something special."

Martin watched as Frank bent over and turned on a switch beneath the crystal stand. It began to rotate slowly. Frank returned to his camera, and every once in a while took another shot.

Ten minutes and two rolls of film later, even Frank was satisfied. "That should be it. If not, maybe they'll reconsider and send us up in a plane. Want to give me a hand closing up shop?"

"Sure."

"Thanks." He started disassembling the nearest light. "Where was I, anyway?"

"How Mr. Carruthers never got upset when you disagreed."

"Yeah, that was Harry's second-best trait, as far as I was concerned. First place went to how good a teacher he was. I owe a lot to that old man." He shook his head sadly. "Sure wish I could have learned some of those lessons without so many hard knocks, though."

"What do you mean?"

"Oh, like what he said about faith. I was a real gung-ho photographer. Got an early break and thought I had the world on a string. Made a bunch of money, spent even more than I made. Got married to this great lady, had a kid, everything was going my way. But I wasn't satisfied. Started fooling around. Real kamikaze stuff. Almost lost it all. I mean, everything. My home, my profession, the works. Walked up to the brink, looked over, thought for the longest time about jumping off."

Frank stopped working. Martin turned from wrapping up electrical cords to find the tall man looking sadly off into the distance. "I hurt a lot of people," Frank said softly.

Martin waited, then asked, "What happened?"

Frank started, as though he had forgotten where he was. "Aw, you don't want to hear all the gory details."

"Yes, I do."

The wounded look returned to Frank's eyes. "The biggest pain you can inflict upon yourself is to hurt someone you love. The worst part about that dark time is that I hurt just about everybody around me."

"You wanted to hurt them?"

Frank Simpson shook his head. "No, I hurt them because I refused to see beyond my own selfish wants. I think that sums it all up, don't you?"

Martin nodded, not sure he really understood what the man was saying, but somehow touched very deeply. Frank Simpson was talking to him as an equal. It was the first time he could ever remember an adult doing that. For a brief instant Martin felt the pain of the past few days slip away.

"I was saved just in time by what I should have learned in the beginning," Frank went on. "Had I learned it when Harry dished it out back in the early days, I could have spared everybody a lot of grief. But I had to learn the hard way that I couldn't make it alone, not and stay on the one true path through life."

"You mean faith," Martin guessed.

Frank Simpson nodded. "The only way for us to give a lasting meaning to this life is to fill it with the Lord's divine love. And that, my friend, is nothing but the undiluted truth."

"You mean," Martin said, "I should ask God to get me back into the photography club?"

"God already knows the desires of your heart," Frank replied. "You need to ask Jesus into your life, and for Him to fill you with the peace that surpasses understanding. You'll never know how important these gifts are—the gift of salvation and the gift of peace—until they live inside your heart."

Monday morning, Martin barely had the energy to get out of bed.

School without the chance to take pictures was just drudgery, as far as he was concerned. But Marge was busy getting ready for her shift and bustling about, and had no patience for him when she decided that he wasn't really sick. She packed him off to school with a brisk kiss.

When he arrived at school, Martin opened his locker, and three slips of paper fluttered down to his feet. He picked them up. The first was from Coach Lynch and said simply, "See me now."

He read the other two on his way to the Industrial Arts classroom. One was from Janice and said, "Don't give up the ship. Reinforcements are arriving."

The third was a dreaded pink slip, which meant he was called to the principal's office. Scribbled on the blank space was the appointment time, 9:30.

Martin pushed through the Industrial Arts door,

hoping desperately that he would not run into either Floyd or Ellen. Coach Lynch looked up from the papers scattered over his desk and barked, "Powell. What took you so long?"

"I just—"

"Never mind." Coach Lynch was already on his feet. "Come out in the hall."

When the door was closed behind them, Coach Lynch said, "Do you have your darkroom key?"

Martin's heart clanged like a broken bell. "Yes."

"Let me have it."

He fished in his pocket and handed it over with benumbed fingers.

"Okay, you better report to class." Coach Lynch turned and walked back into his classroom, leaving Martin standing slumped and sad in the hall. Terribly, terribly sad.

At 9:25 Martin showed his teacher the pink slip and left class. As he walked the empty halls he had a fleeting thought that maybe the principal would do them all a favor and just put him out of his misery.

Mr. Hopkins, the principal, was a very imposing man. He stood somewhere between six and nineteen feet tall and weighed between two and seven hundred pounds—depending upon how closely he loomed over the student, and how mad he was. His voice sounded like a bear in a barrel. Around the halls, among teachers and students alike, the principal's office was known as the Gas Chamber. A meeting with the man was referred to as an execution.

Martin arrived in Mr. Hopkins's office to find

quite a group already waiting. On one side of the room were seated Coach Lynch, Miss Paisley, and Miss Spurles. On the other were Floyd and Ellen. The pair was dressed in black, as usual. Their clothes matched their expressions. They looked like they were going to a funeral. Their own.

"Sit down, Powell," Mr. Hopkins commanded, and pointed to a seat beside Miss Paisley. "There."

Martin did so. His heart hammered in his ears. Miss Paisley gave him a nervous smile. Coach Lynch's habitual frown deepened momentarily. Miss Spurles did not even glance his way. She looked like an old gray-headed tiger ready to pounce, and her prey were seated directly across from her.

"Powell, a certain matter has been brought to my attention," Principal Hopkins said in his sonorous tones. "I do not like such matters disturbing my day. I particularly do not like matters which disrupt the smooth running of such important school projects as our newspaper and yearbook." Beady eyes far too small for Mr. Hopkins's polished dome swiveled to bore into the pair. "Is that absolutely clear?"

Floyd scratched his nose and gave what might have been the smallest nod in human history. Ellen sank another two inches further down in her seat.

"Now these two students have something they wish to say to you," Mr. Hopkins went on, his gaze as penetrating as a dentist's drill. He waited a moment, then roared, "Well?"

Floyd deflated like a popped balloon.

"Iwantyoutocomebackandrejointheclub."

"I'm not sure this student fully understood what

you intended to say to him," Mr. Hopkins rumbled.

Floyd repeated it at a slightly slower pace.

"And you happen to have something there for him, is that not correct?"

Again the tiniest of nods, another moment's hesitation, then Floyd fished into his shirt pocket and handed over the darkroom key, all without looking in Martin's direction.

Martin took the key and resisted the urge to dance across the principal's desk.

"Now then," the principal boomed. "There are a few other items to be discussed, are there not?"

Ellen slid down another notch. Floyd might as well have been carved from some dark stone.

"Firstly, Powell here is granted unlimited use of all equipment in the darkroom, is he not?" The principal leaned his weight across the desk and bore down harder. "And has first right to all camera equipment whenever he wants it. Is that not so?"

Floyd's nod was barely above a shiver. Ellen sank down even further.

"And if there is any further trouble of any kind, you two will lose all darkroom privileges. I will not even ask whose fault it is. At the first peep, you two are banished once and for all. Now is that perfectly clear?"

Floyd gave another shiver. Had Ellen slid another inch farther down in her chair, she would have been lying on the floor.

"Fine." Mr. Hopkins rose to his feet and offered Martin a hand the size of a shovel. "I hope it will not be necessary for you to disturb me again, Powell."

"So do I," Martin replied with heartfelt sincerity,

and watched his hand being swallowed whole.

"But if there is any problem, my door is always open to you," he said, dropping Martin's hand and returning his gaze to the pair struggling to rise. For a moment Martin almost felt sorry for them.

But not for very long.

Martin spent the entire day walking on air.

Janice approached him at lunch hour, took one look, and said, "I guess you've heard."

"About what?"

"About what, the man says. He walks around all week with a face as long as a slow movie, and today he's bouncing like a balloon on the end of a little kid's hand. And he asks me about what."

"Oh. That."

"Yeah, that." Janice sat down beside him. "So how does it feel to bury the terrible twins?"

"I didn't do anything but show up," Martin replied. "You're the one who should feel good."

"I hardly did anything," Janice told him. "I told Miss Paisley, let's see, and Flick, and maybe a couple of others. The ball just started rolling all by itself."

"Well, thanks anyway."

"Anytime," she said, and gave a smile so huge she showed the braces across her back teeth. "It was nice being on the right side for a change."

"What do you mean?"

"You take good pictures. And you're a nice guy. Too nice to have something like this happen to you without a fight. And a lot of people agree."

Martin was busy struggling for something to say when Dan Horner and his two teammates came sauntering over. "Hey, kid, everything all taken care of?"

"See what I mean?" Janice said.

Dan reached down and punched Martin's arm. "I haven't seen the coach so hot since we lost the regionals last year."

"And Miss Spurles," said one of the other guys. "I was in her class when you came by last week. Man, she looked hot enough to chew nails."

"We've got an away game with Broughton this weekend," Dan said. "You coming along for the ride?"

Martin looked a question at Janice, who explained, "It's one of the perks of the job. For away games you get to ride in the team bus."

"Sure," Martin said. "It sounds great."

"Okay, guess we'll see you around, then," Dan said. He punched Martin's shoulder again and sauntered off.

"I guess it's true what they say about clouds and silver linings," Janice said.

"What are you talking about?"

"A lot of people have been forced to choose sides by this," she told him. "Either they were for you, or they let you fall." She smiled. "You wait and see. I'll bet there's a change for the better."

There was. Martin noticed it right off. Almost the entire football team would shout his name as he passed in the halls. People he didn't know nodded and waved in his direction. Girls smiled and said hello.

By Wednesday Mr. Carruthers had recuperated enough for Martin to go by for a brief visit. The old man was seated in his living room with a blanket tucked around his legs, but other than that and a slightly raspy voice, he looked well enough.

Martin sat and sipped at the tea Mrs. Carruthers brought and told him all that had happened. He finished with, "I just wanted to say thanks."

"I have not done a thing," Mr. Carruthers replied, "except pray for you."

"I mean, thanks for making me wait. I can see now that you were right." He explained about the changes he was noticing around school. "Not to mention the fact that I'm boss of the darkroom now."

Mr. Carruthers was silent for a moment, then said, "I am very glad for you. Since my advice appears to have been helpful, may I give you two bits more?"

"Sure," Martin replied. "Anything."

"Thank you. I have always considered giving advice to be a great privilege. A person can show no greater respect to someone than to be willing to listen to something which they might find uncomfortable."

"Mr. Simpson said he could take your advice because you never tried to force it on him."

Mr. Carruthers looked pleased. "I am so glad to hear you have been spending time with Frank. He is a very good man and a very good photographer. The two do not always go hand in hand."

"He also told me he wished he had followed your advice sooner," Martin said.

Mr. Carruthers patted a fold in the blanket. "The next time you see Frank, tell him for me that the Lord restores the years which the locusts have eaten. Will you do that?"

"Sure," Martin said, baffled by the message.

"He can explain it to you if he wishes. All right. My first piece of advice is this: Now is the perfect time to make peace with your enemies, when strength is on your side."

Martin made a face. "I'd rather shake hands with a snake."

"I didn't say make friends with them," Mr. Carruthers replied. "I said, make peace. Defuse any future conflict while the power is in your court."

"Okay," Martin sighed, not liking it, but somehow feeling the sense of it just the same.

"My second bit of advice is as follows: If I have been proven right about this, would you please think on what I have told you about your need for the Lord's help through life?"

Suddenly Martin wanted to be elsewhere. Anywhere would do, just someplace other than there. He rose to his feet. "Sure. I'll think about it."

Mr. Carruthers understood perfectly. "Thank you, Martin. Now go and rejoin the world."

The next morning Martin went by Coach Lynch's office and found the man scribbling plays on his blackboard. Martin knocked on the open door.

"Hey, Powell, what say, what say. Come on in."

"I just wanted to thank you for helping me out."

Coach Lynch nodded approval. "Manners and talent both. You oughtta go far, kid. You plan on going pro?"

"I'd like to," he said quietly, admitting it to himself for the very first time.

The coach's frown deepened, pulling his face into the form of a tired old bulldog. "Well, it's a tough racket from all I've heard. But so is just about anything. If I've ever seen anybody with the gumption to make it, it's you." He fastened Martin with his toughest gaze. "Now get out there and fight, kid. And don't give up 'til you've passed the goalposts."

When Martin entered the Industrial Arts machine

room and saw that the darkroom door was open, he had to steel himself in order to walk further.

Floyd spotted him and stiffened as though caught doing something wrong. Then he forced himself to relax. "Well, well, well. If it isn't the ex-peon. Come to gloat?"

"No." Martin stopped in the doorway. It was as close as he wanted to come.

"Having Coach Cretin on your side gives you a lot of clout with the powers-that-be," Floyd said. "But not with me."

"Me neither," Ellen agreed. She set her black backpack down on the counter with an angry thump and started unloading her camera gear.

"You can keep it," Martin said quietly.

That stopped them both. "What?"

"The thirty-five millimeter cameras," Martin said. "They're yours to use. Both of them. I'll stay with the clunkers."

Joy and relief fought for place on Floyd's features, but he managed to keep them under control. "What," he sneered. "You expect us to be grateful?"

Martin shook his head. "I'm not expecting anything."

"That's good, ex-peon," Floyd snarled. "Because that's exactly what you're going to get. Nothing. Come on, Ellen. It's starting to stink in here."

Hastily, Ellen stuffed her gear back into her pack, as though fearful Martin might change his mind. But as she left the old Ellen was back in control. "Everything he said," she told him, "in spades."

Martin watched them leave, feeling a little

shaky from the contact. Yet despite the charged atmosphere they left behind, he still felt that what he had done was right. Which somehow left him feeling under pressure to consider what the old man had said about faith.

And that left him more unsettled than ever.

Martin arrived at Mr. Singer's shop that afternoon only to hear the old man say, "The mischief-maker has called. He wants you at his studio."

"Who, Mr. Simpson?"

"Mister, is it now? The mischief-maker does not deserve to be called mister." The little man peered at Martin. "Something has happened, yes?"

Martin nodded. "I'm back in the darkroom again."

"So, the world has not ended after all. What do you know?" The little man shooed him towards the door. "Go, go, the light on your face would blind customers. Go and let the mischief-maker see if he can keep you busy today."

The warehouse door was swung open by an elfin sprite with close-cropped auburn hair and a brilliant smile. "Are you Martin?"

Martin felt his heart give a slight lurch. He nodded a yes.

"Great. I'm Cindy Simpson." She stuck out her hand. "My dad's been talking about you so much I decided to come down and take a look for myself." She cocked her head to one side and made a silly face. "Funny, you don't look like a genius."

Martin felt as though his mind was mired in bubble gum. "Mr. Simpson is your father?"

"Yeah. Didn't he mention me?"

Martin shook his head.

"Figures." She turned and bounced up the stairs. "Come on up. Dad's going crazy."

"Martin, great, not a moment too soon." Frank turned from the two models lounging on the neutral-colored stage. "Start loading up all those lights in the van downstairs, okay? Soon as we're finished with this I want to go do a shoot by the fountain in front of city hall."

Cindy walked over to the pile of equipment with Martin and hefted a coil of cable that looked heavier than she was. "Dad's been going nuts, worrying that it's gonna rain or something before we're ready. The fact that there hasn't been a single cloud spotted anywhere in America all day doesn't matter."

"With my luck," Frank said, scuttling over to the other model and adjusting the way she stood, "there'll be a tornado the minute we step outside."

"That makes perfect sense to me," the auburn-haired pixie said to Martin. "Doesn't that make sense to you?"

"Okay, ladies," Frank Simpson said, returning to stand behind his camera. "Now give me your very best smile, please."

Cindy responded by facing Martin on the stairs, crossing her eyes, sticking her tongue in the side of her mouth, and giving a lopsided leer.

Martin almost tripped over his own feet, and came within inches of doing a head over heels down the stairs.

"What," Cindy asked innocently. "Do I make you nervous?"

Martin raced down the stairs, dumped his load of light stands into the van, and fled back upstairs.

Cindy tripped lightly along behind him. "Dad's assistant is still sick, as usual. That guy spends more time in bed than a pillow. Dad likes to use me, but I swim for the Eastwood team, and practice takes up a lot of my afternoons."

Martin hefted a case of lights, and asked, "You go to Eastwood?"

"Didn't I just say that?" Cindy looked over to where her father was turning the two models so that they faced each other. The brunette wore a white outfit, the blond an identical black outfit. They had their hair tied up in identical styles with ribbons to match their outfits. They wore identically bored expressions. "Didn't I just say that, Pater?"

Frank Simpson muttered something inaudible and stepped back to check his work.

"Poor Daddy," Cindy whispered, dropping her voice to a level only Martin could hear. "He gets so preoccupied when he has to work with munchkins. And two of them at once is almost more than he can handle."

Martin stumbled towards the door and said, "Munchkins?"

"Are you going to parrot everything I say?" Cindy demanded, traipsing down the stairs behind him. "Because if you are it's going to be a very tedious afternoon."

Martin dropped his case into the van with a groan. "Sorry."

"Sorry, the man says. Okay, let's take it from the top." She set down her load and stuck out her hand. "Cindy Simpson. How terrifically delightful to make your acquaintance."

Martin grinned. "I bet you don't give Mr. Singer that lip."

"What, dear old Uncle Joseph? He's a pussycat."

Martin had to laugh. "Don't ever let him hear you call him that."

"Don't worry. My daddy didn't raise no fool." Cindy returned his grin. "Come on, Pater's going to be ready to roll in about thirty seconds."

The city's main administrative building was fronted by a great plaza, part of an attempt to restore the downtown sector. The plaza contained a broad fountain. In its center rose a tall modern-art sculpture which reminded Martin of an old-fashioned washboard. Water ran continually over its polished surface. Sunlight was reflected off the running water, the washboard, and the pool. With the deep blue sky overhead, the plaza made an impressive setting for an outdoor fashion shoot.

It was Martin's first public session, and nothing could have prepared him for the crowd that quickly gathered. He tried as hard as he could to follow Cindy's and Frank's and the models' examples, and ignore it all. But it was impossible. The lights were set up, and the park attendant unlocked the outdoor receptacle for them to plug in their equipment. By the time the big screens used to soften and spread the light were set into place, at least fifty people had gathered. The park attendants were kept busy making sure nobody got in the way. Cindy fussed over the models, who had the ability to look blankly at nothing while they were being positioned. Frank moved at a frantic pace, pointing Martin towards a light, racing up to help Cindy adjust how the models were standing, running back to check through the viewfinder, then back again, muttering to himself, glancing continually at the sky. Frank was clearly a very worried man.

The models were beautiful. Martin saw how the entire crowd's attention, especially the men's, remained fastened on the blond and the brunette. Their makeup was perfect, their hairstyles were immaculate, their clothes shiny and new. And when Frank was ready and standing behind the camera and talking to the models directly, they posed with grace and flair and flashed brilliant smiles.

But Martin could not get enough of Cindy.

She moved with the delicacy of a hummingbird, touching down only for an instant, then dancing away. Her hair lifted and spun in time to her movements. Martin watched her and decided he had never seen anyone who looked so alive.

The afternoon passed swiftly. When the sun touched the nearby buildings and sent shadows out across the park, the crowd began to disperse. Frank Simpson thanked the models and sent them home by taxi. Cindy's gay chatter kept them company as they loaded up the equipment and drove back to the studio.

When the van was unloaded she spun on a dancer's foot and announced, "I am so late Mom will probably ground me for life."

"Tell her it was my fault," Frank offered.

"She knows it's your fault, Daddy dear," Cindy replied. "It's always your fault. Mom doesn't need anybody telling her that."

"No, I suppose not," Frank said, rolling his eyes at Martin.

"The day you arrive home on time is the day Mom drops down in a dead faint."

"That's enough, daughter."

Cindy turned to Martin. "Did you know that he actually—"

"Cindy," Frank growled a warning.

"Well, I suppose I better go. No reason to get both parents mad at me. Not at the same time, anyway." She cocked her head and examined Martin, then decided, "Pater, I've decided that I approve."

"Well, that is certainly a relief," Frank said, storing his cameras one at a time in the metal shelves with the combination lock.

Martin asked, "Approve of what?"

"Of you, silly," Cindy replied. "Daddy, you now have permission to ask him."

Frank began writing labels for each roll of film. "My daughter is usually content with an equal say in our household. Sometimes she wants more, though, and that's when I have to get tough."

"Tough. Right. Old Daddykins the tiger. Watch me tremble."

"Quiet, you. Otherwise I might dock your pay."

Cindy slapped a hand across her mouth and spoke her reply through her fingers.

"As I was saying, she is an equal partner in many of our family decisions. It is part of learning to live with a fairly grown-up daughter in the house."

"Who someday will inherit her father's studio, right, Daddy?"

"You want to be a photographer too?" Martin demanded.

"It is very doubtful on some days," Frank Simpson replied, "that my daughter will live that long."

"What Pater was working his way towards and would probably get around to saying within the next year or so," Cindy said, then had to stop and breathe, "was that we're taking a photography expedition to Florida after Christmas. And Daddy got it in his head that he wanted to ask you to come along."

"Me?"

"Don't interrupt, it's not nice. My mother, being an extremely intelligent person, not to mention beautiful, after whom I take in every department except talent with a camera—" she paused for a smug smile "—insisted that I act as emissary and come down to make sure you didn't drool or drag your knuckles on the ground." She made a worried face. "You don't, do you?"

Martin looked from one to the other. "You want me to come with you to Florida?"

"Leave by car Christmas Day," Frank Simpson said. "Arrive back the day before school begins."

"Three days in the Everglades taking pictures of everything that crawls, walks, or flies. A night launch of the space shuttle unless they forget to hit one of the switches, and a day on a boat trying to take pictures while seasick." Cindy intertwined her fingers. "Say yes, please, okay?"

How well do you know these people?" Marge asked, when he told her about the invitation that evening.

"They're friends," Martin replied. "Good friends. Can I go?"

Instead of answering, she looked at him across the dinner table. Her expression was solemn. Then she asked, "Don't you think maybe you're becoming a little too involved in this photography business?"

"No," he replied defensively. "Not at all."

"There's so much more to life," she went on firmly. "You're young, there's a whole world out there for you to explore."

"That's exactly what I'm doing," Martin said, trying hard to keep from getting angry. He knew from experience that if he got mad, he lost. And this was too important to lose. "I'm learning about the world."

"But through the lens of a camera," she persisted.

"Doesn't it seem like, well, maybe you're trying to put a barrier between yourself and the rest of the world?"

Hard as he tried, he could feel his own control slipping away. "Why did we sell our house and move across town, Mom?"

That caught her totally off guard. "What?"

"After the funeral," he said, then had to stop and swallow hard. "It felt like you couldn't get away from home fast enough."

"I told you," she said, her voice suddenly shaky. "We needed to make a new beginning."

"You needed to," Martin corrected. His chest hurt from the growing pressure. "I wanted to stay right where I was."

"Why didn't you say anything?"

"I tried," he said, and had to swallow again. "But you weren't listening so good right then. And I didn't know what to say. Maybe you were right. But I didn't think so. And I still don't."

"Well." She gave a shaky sigh. "We can't go backwards."

"No," he said, and was startled by a sense of suddenly seeing the whole world from a different perspective.

It was not that he stopped seeing the room and the dining table and his mother. It was as though he was seeing that on the outside and something else within himself. He knew a moment of inner clarity.

The world was rushing by so fast, so full of changes. So many things that were totally out of his control. He was growing up. He was in a new house and a new neighborhood and a new world of high school. Everything rushing by, and all he could do was try to keep up.

"I don't see what this has to do with what we were talking about," his mother said.

"It has everything to do with it," he replied, but for the moment he was still busy trying to figure out what he was seeing in his mind's eye. It was like, it was like. . . . Martin struggled to make sense of the image. Then he understood. It was as if he were able to take a tiny segment of his world, his high-speed, ever-changing world, and with his camera bring it into focus. Stop it. Hold on to it. Make it real. Make it clear.

Make it his.

"We were talking about your photography," his mother said. "Not some decision that was made over a year ago."

"I'm trying to deal with everything the best I can," Martin replied, more certain of this than he had been of anything since, since. . . .

Since his father had died.

But all he said was, "I think I know what I want to do with my life."

Marge's eyes widened. "Become a photographer?"

Martin shook his head. "I'm already a photographer, Mom."

"What then?"

Martin looked at her square on and replied, "Become a professional photographer."

You've changed," Janice announced a few weeks later.

They were huddled together during a Friday afternoon assembly, down on the front row with some of the class big shots and a couple of teachers, trying very hard to stay awake. The senior class president was giving a speech about the upcoming Turkey Day Festivities. The activities took place every year the day before the Thanksgiving recess and were always a lot of fun. But the senior class president had a voice as bland as oatmeal. He talked on one single note, sort of sending half the air up through his nose so that it sounded as though he had swallowed a kazoo. The gym was utterly silent, quieter even than when the principal talked, because almost all the students were fighting to keep their eyes open. On Janice's other side, Flick was snoring quietly.

So nobody paid Martin any attention when he

whispered back, "What do you mean?"

"Since the battle with the terrible twins," Janice said quietly. "You're different."

"How different?"

She thought about that and decided, "More determined."

Martin considered what she had said. He had not seen the pair since that day. They came and went like shadows, using the darkroom when he was not there. The only evidence of their passage was the messes they left behind. They never cleaned up a thing.

Martin looked out to where the senior class president droned on endlessly. Even the principal, seated in his high-backed chair behind the podium, was having trouble fighting off a case of the drowsies. No, Martin decided, it was not the argument with Floyd and Ellen that had changed him. It was everything.

Since the night of the talk with his mother, Martin had found himself devoting more and more time to the photography. Every spare minute was spent with Mr. Carruthers or in Mr. Singer's shop or at Mr. Simpson's studio. The only reason he paid attention to his homework was the feeling that if he let his grades slip he would give his mother an excuse to make him cut back. When his grade card came back with almost all B's, he thought he saw a shadow of disappointment cross Marge's face, but it came and went so fast he couldn't be sure.

Things were running much smoother now. The cameras fit him like a second set of hands. He handled a light meter without conscious thought.

He was learning to anticipate. And his pictures were showing the result.

At the last game, Martin had captured a shot of Kevin Murphy leaping over a bunched and struggling line for the winning touchdown. The local newspaper had called the day the school paper came out, and offered to take him on as a stringer.

"A what?" Martin had replied.

"Stringer," the man repeated. He had a voice shaped by too many cigarettes smoked for too many years. "Drop your negatives here after every game. We'll develop them for free, take a look at what you got. Pay you fifty bucks for any shot we use. How's that sound?"

That had been two days ago. Martin was still repeating the word to himself when he was alone. Stringer.

After school Martin stopped by the Carruthers home on his way to the shop. By now it was an established routine. Mr. Carruthers greeted him with, "I have been thinking about what you should work on next."

"I've got just about everything I can handle," Martin pointed out.

"And you are getting too comfortable," Mr. Carruthers replied. "Things are becoming a little too easy for you."

"I wouldn't say that," Martin protested. "Not at all. It's a lot of work."

"Easy I said and easy I mean. You are beginning to master the work involved with action photography." Mr. Carruthers held up his hand to stop Martin from replying. "Yes, yes, I know there is still a lot to learn. But you are comfortable with it. And sometimes learning can only come from what I like to call the action of the pearl."

Martin cocked his head so as to look at the old man from the corner of his eye. He had no idea where Mr. Carruthers was headed, but something told him he was not going to like it when they got there.

"An oyster can sit for years and years on the bottom of the sea, doing nothing but existing, going nowhere at all. Then a tiny bit of sand works itself inside the shell. The sand is an irritant. It threatens the oyster's existence. So the oyster begins working with that sand, coating it with the same lining it uses on the inside of its shell. And in the end you have a beautiful pearl."

"It sounds painful," Martin observed.

"Growth sometimes is," Mr. Carruthers replied.

"So what do you have in mind?"

Mr. Carruthers fastened him with a penetrating gaze. "Have you given any thought to what I said to you about faith?"

Martin became even more uncomfortable than he already was. "Sure. Some. A little."

"And?"

"And I don't know. I guess I feel like I'm doing pretty okay on my own."

"Comfortable," Mr. Carruthers repeated. "It is a dangerous state to be in sometimes. And I intend to challenge that, my young friend."

"Like how?"

"Like by starting you on a new assignment."

Martin made a face. "Can't it wait?"

Mr. Carruthers shook his head. "Not an instant longer. Tell me, what else are you working on at school besides taking pictures of the games?"

Martin shrugged. "The usual stuff. Oh, and I'm supposed to get some close-ups of the movers and shakers for the yearbook. You know, the class president and the cheerleaders and the girl who won the state math prize. Stuff like that."

"Perfect," Mr. Carruthers cried. "I could not have asked for anything better."

"Than shooting some pictures of people?" Martin was confused. "What's so great about that?"

"Great is precisely the word," Mr. Carruthers replied. He leaned forward in his chair. "My boy, I want you to search for the unseen."

"Do what?"

"Go beyond the superficial," Mr. Carruthers continued. "Look for the hidden. Seek out the beautiful. The meaningful."

Mr. Carruthers leaned back, utterly satisfied. "And I want you to learn from what you find."

Martin started off with the cheerleaders. He figured they would be easiest. If beautiful was what Mr. Carruthers wanted, beautiful would be what he got.

Only he was totally dissatisfied with the results. And he couldn't figure out why.

Martin shot four entire rolls. First he did the cheerleaders as a group, standing and smiling, then doing jumps and twists and pirouettes and pyramids. Then he did a series of photos of one after the other. He finished up by taking a page from Frank Simpson's book, by pairing the blond-haired Nancy Starling with a dark-haired beauty. He shot them standing back to back with their pompons raised waist-high. He shot them holding hands and leaning back, their hair spilling down behind them, the pompons littered like flowers at their feet. He shot them close up, smiling beautifully, with the school emblem directly behind them.

He spent hours poring over the results, trying to figure out what was wrong.

The cheerleaders themselves were ecstatic with the results. He even got kissed on the cheek by two of them, which for some reason just made it worse. Flick swallowed his smirk about halfway through the pile, which made Janice heat up and stomp away.

Everybody was pleased except him.

He told Cindy about it that night by phone. They were talking almost every night. She was incredibly busy with swimming and school, and did not make it to the studio more than once every couple of weeks. But whenever she did, Martin made it a point to be there. Her only free evening was Saturdays, which was when he had the football games, and she was adamant that she was not going to spend her only free night watching him work. Besides, she told him, she hated football. So they tied up the phone lines, and saw each other from time to time, and looked forward to both the Florida trip and to the swim season ending in February.

When Martin had explained the problem as best he could, Cindy was quiet for a long moment. Then she said, "Daddy always likes to talk to them."

"Who?"

"People he's doing portraits of. He says it makes them relax and builds an atmosphere."

Martin looked back in his mind. "They all seemed relaxed to me. They were laughing and everything."

"I don't know," Cindy replied. "But he says it helps a lot. Maybe you should give it a try."

The next day he was supposed to photograph Kevin Murphy, the school's star quarterback and captain of the team. Kevin showed up twenty minutes late, his hair still wet from practice. "Sorry," he said. "The coach kept us late."

"That's okay," Martin said. He could see that Kevin was nervous. Edgy. He kept shooting worried glances at the camera in Martin's hand. Martin pointed to a chair he had taken from behind the teacher's desk and set in the afternoon light streaming through the window. "Why don't you go over there and sit down?"

"In the coach's chair?" Kevin gave a nervous laugh. "Promise he won't make me run laps?"

"What's the matter?" Martin asked, squatting and focusing for the first picture. "I take your picture all the time."

"I know," Kevin said, trying not to wince as the flash went off. "But this is different."

"Different how?"

"I don't know, just different. Out on the field I guess maybe I'm too busy to think about anything else."

Martin slid over a notch and raised his camera again. "Or maybe you're more comfortable when you're hiding behind all that padding."

"Yeah, right." This time the laugh was a little

more genuine. "Maybe I should go get my helmet."

Martin captured the laugh on film and tried to keep the conversation going. "What else do you do besides football?"

"Not much. Try to stay in school. I want to run track in the spring."

"Hey, me too." Another picture. "You have any brothers or sisters?"

"One sister, Margaret. You've probably seen her around."

"I don't think so."

Kevin was looking out the window, more relaxed now. Less self-conscious. "Yeah, she's pretty quiet."

"What does your dad do?"

At that there was a hint of something in Kevin's eyes. "Fight with my mom." Then it was pushed aside, and a fakey grin was set in its place. "What a lousy thing to say. I guess that makes me a creep, right?"

Martin kept taking pictures, knowing that he could not use them, but wanting to keep the rhythm going. "I think you're a really nice guy."

"Shows how much you know." Kevin looked down, as though ignoring the camera and seeing just Martin. "What about you?"

"Photography's my life," he said simply. Click.

"Yeah, I guess I could see that for myself. You do great work."

"Thanks."

"I don't know anything about you except that you take pictures. What about your family?"

"I'm an only child. My mother's a nurse." Click.

And then it just came out. Naturally. Painlessly. "My father's dead."

"Hey, that's tough. What happened?"

"He had a heart attack last year." Martin lowered the camera far enough to be able to look over it. But he was really concentrating on what was going on inside. It was the first time he had ever just talked about it. "It was totally sudden. We didn't even know he was sick or anything. He was only forty-seven."

The bloom of something deep returned to Kevin's eyes. "Sometimes I wish. . . ." He let the sentence die unspoken. Then he lowered his head, as though the sorrow that came to his eyes was so heavy he could not keep his head upright.

Martin clicked the camera, and Kevin was so caught up in his internal sorrow that he did not notice. Martin saw that the line of his face was all wrong. Why he could not say, but it was wrong. There was something missing. He wondered how it would be if Kevin raised his head, took out the folds in his neck. But he could not ask, because he sensed that if he did it would spoil the moment, and the curtains in Kevin's eyes would descend.

So he said quietly, "The sky sure is pretty this time of day."

And Kevin raised his head. "Yeah, guess so," he said quietly, his gaze still achingly open.

Martin took the picture. And another. And a third.

Then Kevin brought the world back into focus, turned to Martin, and said, "How much more do you need?"

Martin dropped his camera and wished there was something he could do or say. Something that might repay the openness that Kevin had shared through his eyes. Something to help ease his pain. But Martin had nothing. So all he said was, "That's enough. Thanks. Thanks a lot."

For the first time since meeting Mr. Carruthers, Martin did not want to share his discovery with the old man. Not then, not yet.

Instead, the afternoon that he developed the picture of Kevin Murphy, he took two cross-town buses and hiked the half mile or so to Cindy's house. He sat on the curb, the house blocked from view by an ancient oak, and waited for her to come home.

He heard her before he saw her. The late afternoon was unseasonably mild. Cindy's gay chatter suddenly drifted in as a car pulled up and stopped. Martin stood and waited while she laughed her way from the car, suddenly uncertain, wondering if maybe he had done the wrong thing.

Cindy waved her friends off, turned, spotted him standing there, and lit the dusk with her smile. "Martin! What are you doing here?"

"I wanted to show you something," he said, as

always feeling tongue-tied and stumble-footed around her.

"Come on inside," she said, and reached for his hand.

He dug in his heels. "I'd rather not."

She stopped and looked up at him. "What's the matter?"

"Nothing's the matter. I just don't want anybody else to see this." Shyly he opened the manila folder in his hands and pulled out the picture. Cindy drew up close to him. When the photograph came into view, she gave a quick little intake of breath.

Kevin Murphy had his head lifted so that his face pointed directly towards the unseen light. His gaze seemed to search infinity for an answer to that which troubled him so. There was little hope in that face, but incredible strength. And determination. Kevin Murphy faced an unseen future with a resolve that no matter what, he would do his best and give his all.

"Who is he?" Cindy finally asked.

"The school quarterback."

"Why does he look like that?"

"I don't know him all that well. But it sounds like his parents are having problems."

"You talked to him?"

Martin nodded, then realized that she could not see his movement, because her attention remained centered upon the picture. "Yes."

"Can I have it?"

"I guess so," Martin said, not wanting to refuse her anything.

She looked up at the uncertainty in his voice. "What's wrong?"

Martin reddened. "I'm just not all that excited about you having another guy's picture," he confessed.

To his surprise, she did not laugh at him. Instead, her grip on his hand tightened. She raised up on tiptoe and kissed him lightly on the cheek. "I better go inside. Mom's probably worried that there was a kidnapper hiding behind the tree."

"Little does she know," Martin said, and held out the picture.

"You keep it," Cindy replied. "Just let me come over and look at it again, okay?"

"Any time you like."

She hesitated, then asked, "Would you like to come to church with me on Sunday?"

That stopped him. "Church?"

"Oh, dear." Cindy made a face. "Not that parrot again. I did so enjoy talking with a real human being."

Martin thought of what Mr. Carruthers had said, and replied, "Church sounds okay."

"Great. You can come over for breakfast and meet my mom." She danced to the front step, spun, and called back, "You are going to be a great artist, Martin Powell. G'night."

Friday arrived, and he was still not ready to share his discovery with Mr. Carruthers. On some basic level he knew that the old man would present him with another challenge, some unseen next step. And right then it was all still too new. He was able to visualize it through the lens, but he was still not sure of what he was seeing. Or why.

Instead of heading to Mr. Carruthers and then to the shop, Martin hung around the darkroom long after the place was clean. He was unsure of what he wanted or needed to do. He continued straightening things that were already in order. Enjoying his aloneness. Sorting through the jumble in his head.

A banging clatter in the classroom outside made him jump. He peered through the door, saw that it was Mr. Jenkins the janitor. Something made him pick up his camera before going out to say hello.

Mr. Jenkins gave a little start when Martin popped into view. "Hey there, boy. What're you doing around here?"

"Just cleaning up a little."

"Yeah, you and me both." He started shifting around chairs and sweeping the floor with great practiced motions. "Young kid like you, figured the last place you'd wanna be on a Friday afternoon is cooped up here with us chickens."

"I guess I don't think of the darkroom as school," Martin said, raising the camera and focusing.

Mr. Jenkins stopped cold. "What're you doing with that thing?"

"Just practicing," Martin said, clicking the shutter.

"Hmph." He went back to his sweeping. "You and old Harry Carruthers. Always sticking that picture-box into every little place you can imagine."

"You and Mr. Carruthers were friends, weren't

you?" Martin found it easier to talk and shoot this time. He crouched down, hoping it would make him sort of disappear. Wondering why he was taking these pictures at all.

"Yeah, that old Harry, he's some kinda guy." Mr. Jenkins reached for the trash can, rapped it into his wheeled collector with a bang. "Always had a kind word, always time for a little chat. Treated a man like a man, if you know what I mean."

"I like him too," Martin said, taking another picture.

"Yeah, I could see that right off, how you two got along. Wasn't every student down here, got a key to the school. No sir, I could count the students he wheedled a key off me for on the fingers of one hand."

"How long have you been working at Westover?" Click.

"Since the day the school opened," Mr. Jenkins said with a chuckle. "Yessir, been sweeping these floors long as the floors've been here." He stopped with his sweeping, leaned his weight heavy on the handle. "Came back from Korea, jobs were right scarce. Felt kinda lucky to get this. Guess it just grew on me."

Martin focused again, realized Mr. Jenkins's face was too far in the shadows. He looked up, saw how the light was angling in from the left. As quietly as he could, Martin eased himself over, then crouched down low and spoke again, hoping that the changed direction of his voice would draw the man's head around. "You've seen a lot of kids come and go, haven't you?"

Mr. Jenkins laughed again, a rusty sound. "Shoot, I've seen stuff that'd curl your toes. Nobody ever sees the janitor. I've stood around these halls and watched 'em come, watched 'em grow up or run away, watched 'em leave. Could almost point out the ones that'd make it and those that wouldn't."

Martin hesitated, not wanting to click the shutter, not yet. He felt like he was on the brink of something, and searched for a way forward. "What would you say is the biggest difference between those who made it and those who didn't?"

The heart's door opened. The face softened. The lines eased from their perpetual scowl into those of a tired hard-working man who somehow had managed to hold onto both his humor and his character.

"Man's got to be honest with himself," Mr. Jenkins replied quietly. "Makes all the difference in the world. Ups and downs are gonna come in this life. Bound to. But if a man ain't honest he'll never enjoy the good times or the good things. World's fulla people who think they're up, but all they're doing is going through the motions. Can't think of anything sadder than somebody who's made it on the outside and failed on the inside."

Martin took his picture, wound the film, took another, and listened. Despite his busy hands, he felt the janitor's words echo down deep inside himself.

"You see 'em building those walls of lies as they walk these very halls," Mr. Jenkins said, his gaze on students that had come and gone long before. "Life hits 'em hard, and they decide to run away inside themselves. Drugs or sex or clubs or good-time buddies or grins that don't mean a thing. Fact is, they're scared, and they're trying to run away. But you can't run away from something that's inside yourself, now, can you?"

"No," Martin replied quietly.

" 'Course not. Honesty's the key. And like a lot of things, man's gotta be honest with himself before he can be honest with others. Hard to be that strong. Only place I know to find that sorta strength is in God."

Mr. Jenkins drew the world back into focus and glanced at the wall clock. "Lookit the time. I keep jawing, I'm gonna miss my dinner." He set his broom into place and wheeled his cart out of the room. "Be seeing you around, kid."

Martin eased himself from his crouch, rewound the film, and flicked the catch on the camera's side. As he pulled out the exposed roll, he looked around. The walls seemed to vibrate from the power of the janitor's words.

Breakfast with the Simpsons was a riotous affair.
Cindy's mother was as sharp as her daughter. "So
you are the young man my family talks about
constantly." She cocked her head to one side.
"Strange. I thought you would be about eleven feet
tall, from everything they've said."

"He's short, but he's strong," Cindy said,
bouncing into view, and smiling up at him. "Hi."

"I am not short," Martin retorted.

"Well, petite doesn't sound right," Cindy said.
"How about sprightly?"

"How about you two let him into the house?"
Frank Simpson said, pushing the two women aside
and offering Martin his hand. "You have to learn
just to ignore ninety percent of everything they say.
It's the only way to stay sane around here."

"Don't listen to Daddy," Cindy said. "He's
always in a bad mood on Sundays. He thinks ties
cut off the blood circulation to his head."

"I don't think, I know," Frank replied, leading Martin into the dining room. The table was laden with a breakfast for ten. "Ties are for people who need to keep their heads from floating away."

"I think you look marvelous in a tie," Mrs. Simpson said. "And I wish you would wear one more often. Sit down here, Martin. Do you like pancakes?"

"Yes, Ma'am."

"Listen to that," Mrs. Simpson said. "Manners. How wonderful. You must come around here more often and teach them to my daughter."

"Too late," Cindy said, carrying a plate piled high with breakfast sausages in from the kitchen. "I'm already done the way I am."

"Cindy tells me you have taken another remarkable picture," Frank Simpson said.

"Daddy," Cindy complained, and when Martin looked her way she explained, "He forced it out of me with pliers and tongs."

"Don't be silly," Frank said. "I merely noticed that my daughter was looking starry-eyed through dinner, and I asked her why."

"I don't ever look starry-eyed," Cindy retorted.

There was the sound of someone coughing in the kitchen.

"Are you all right in there, Mummy?" Cindy asked.

"I brought a couple of pictures with me," Martin said.

"Great," Frank Simpson said. "Let's see them."

Shyly Martin brought out the picture of Kevin Murphy and handed it over. Cindy crowded up behind her father. Frank Simpson looked at it for a long moment, then without raising his head he called, "Angie, can you come in here for a moment?"

"Just for a second," she said, hurrying over. "Otherwise they'll burn." She stepped up behind her husband, looked down, and said, "Oh, my."

Martin reached into his envelope, and slid out one more. "I took this one Friday."

Frank Simpson set the photograph of Mr. Jenkins down beside the one of Kevin Murphy. The janitor's face was an incredible mixture of strength and softness. Ancient lines dug deep crevices in his face. But the eyes glowed with a humorous light.

Frank looked up and said quietly, "You are developing at a remarkable pace."

"These—" Mrs. Simpson started. "The pancakes!"

"Who is he?" Cindy asked, staying where she was.

"The janitor at our school."

"I like these," Frank Simpson said. "Very much."

"Sit down, everybody," Mrs. Simpson said. "These have to be eaten while they're hot."

After Martin had been stuffed like the Christmas turkey, they took him to church. He sat through the service, more aware of Cindy's nearness than of what the preacher said. But she remained caught up in what was going on, so Martin did his best to pay attention.

When the service was over, they drove him back home. As they pulled up in front of his house, Martin was struck by an idea. It hit him with a force that seemed propelled by something outside himself.

He realized that Cindy was staring at him. She said, "You suddenly got one of those preoccupied looks, the kind Daddy has when he's working on a project."

Martin was not used to being read so closely. It both warmed and unsettled him. He turned to the front seat and said, "My mom wants to know if you can come over for dinner one night."

"She wants to see who it is that's taking her son off to the wilds of Florida," Cindy interpreted.

"Quiet, daughter," Mrs. Simpson said. "Please thank your mother for us, and tell her we'd be delighted."

Frank turned in his seat and said, "I can't get those pictures of yours out of my mind."

"Me neither," Cindy agreed.

Martin climbed from the car. "Thanks a lot for everything."

Mrs. Simpson reached out of her window and patted his hand. "I am so glad my husband and daughter found you and brought you home."

"Mother," Cindy complained. "You make him sound like a stray dog."

Mrs. Simpson ignored her and went on, "Tell your mother that I'll call her this week. And you be sure to come visit us again very soon."

Frank leaned across his wife and said, "I was going to speak with you about this after our trip, but I suppose I might as well mention it now. How would you like to come help me in the studio on a regular basis?"

"Daddy's assistant is a permanent drip," Cindy said. "I mean, he has one."

"It would mean giving up your work at Mr. Singer's store," Frank warned.

"He'll probably have something to say about Daddy being a horrible influence and all that," Cindy went on. "But I didn't turn out all that bad, did I?"

"We'd work it out for you to come in three afternoons a week and all day Saturday," Frank said. "It'll mean a lot of work, but I guarantee you would be learning and helping me out."

"I'd like that," Martin said, "more than I know how to say."

Cindy rewarded him with a smile. "How utterly great."

"We'll iron out the details in the New Year," Frank said, and offered Martin his hand through the window.

Martin watched them drive away, then went into the house. His mother was working the day shift, so was not at home. He went upstairs, picked up the Hasselblad, and left again. The force of the idea lingered on, pushing him to action.

When he arrived at Mr. Carruthers's house and rang the bell, Mrs. Carruthers was both pleased to see him and worried. "Oh dear, hello, young man. I'm afraid Mr. Carruthers is not to be disturbed. It's the sabbath, you see."

"I know," Martin said. "But I have to see him just the same. Tell him it's important. Please."

"Oh, well, I suppose if it's important," she said. "Wait right there, please."

In a moment she returned and opened the door for him. "He's in the living room."

Mr. Carruthers did not rise as Martin entered the room. He saw the camera in Martin's hand and gave a very small smile. "I see," he said quietly.

"Please just go ahead with what you were doing," Martin said.

He patted the Bible open in his lap. "I was reading and thinking. Shall I tell you what I was thinking about?"

"That would be great," Martin said, wondering if there would be enough light in the room for him to shoot without a flash. "Do you mind if I open the drapes a little?"

"Be my guest." When Mrs. Carruthers poked her head into the room, Mr. Carruthers said, "Everything is fine, my dear. Martin will be here with me for a while."

When the door was closed once more, Mr. Carruthers said, "I was reading from the tenth chapter of Hebrews. And I was thinking how we are like rechargeable batteries. We must continually return to commune with God and recharge our spiritual life. Do you know what I mean?"

"I'm not sure," Martin replied. He moved around the room turning on all the lights, then watched how they altered the shadows and lines on the old gentleman's face. It was the first time he had ever been able to work with a subject and adjust the lighting before beginning to shoot.

"Before Jesus came to live here on earth," Mr. Carruthers went on, "the temple in Jerusalem was divided by a series of barriers. The men went here, the women there. There was a third room for foreign worshipers. And there was another chamber entirely for God."

Martin saw how the standing lamp situated

behind Mr. Carruthers cast one side of his face in light and the other in shadow. Quietly he drew the lamp up closer, so that both of the eyes would be illuminated. He adjusted it another fraction, trying to keep the light on the eyes while still having a touch of shadow on the face.

"God's room was called the Most Holy Place," Mr. Carruthers continued. "It was separated by a cloth barrier, a great heavy curtain that fell something like fifty feet and ran from wall to wall. Only the chief priest could enter God's room, and only once a year."

Satisfied, Martin dropped to his knees before the old man's chair, and held up his light meter.

"But at the moment when Jesus died on the cross," Mr. Carruthers said, looking down at Martin and yet seeing somewhere far beyond him, "that great curtain was split right in two. From ceiling to floor. It was torn right in half."

I want to capture that light in his eyes, Martin thought to himself. Somehow he was caught up in the picture-taking and the story both. He raised the camera and focused.

"What does this mean?" Mr. Carruthers asked. "Why did the Lord split the curtain at that very moment? I will tell you. The torn curtain was a symbol. It meant that the barriers no longer existed between man and God. And there was a message. Can you guess what the message was?"

Martin started to take the picture, then hesitated. Something held him back. His finger on the shutter, he said, "That we should go inside?"

"Exactly!" And Mr. Carruthers looked down at him, directly through the camera lens, into Martin's eyes and through his eyes into his soul. The light in Mr. Carruthers's gaze illuminated the recesses of Martin's heart as he clicked the shutter.

"We must draw near to God," Mr. Carruthers said, his eyes shining. "We must pause in our lives and walk the bridge that Jesus has built for us with His sacrifice. We must enter into the Most Holy Place with prayer and thanksgiving, and let God work His wonders in our lives."

They left for Florida on Christmas Day and drove all night long. The interstate stretched out in front of their car like an endless concrete ribbon. As the hours passed, the two women grew steadily quieter. Finally only Martin and Frank were still awake.

They rode in silence for a while, then Frank gave a deep satisfied sigh and said quietly, "Times like these, I feel like God's granted me the greatest riches a man could have. A super wife, great daughter, work I love. All the problems just sort of fade away. I think maybe that's why I've always loved driving at night like this. Gives me time to think, see things more in perspective."

Martin opened his mouth to reply, then remembered. "I forgot something."

"What's that?"

"I was supposed to pass on a message from Mr. Carruthers," Martin said. "It was after our conversation about religion."

"Faith," Frank corrected.

"Right," Martin agreed, and wondered why he had such trouble with that word. "Anyway, I told him what you said about wishing you could have learned those lessons earlier. He said for you to remember that. . . ." Martin stopped and scrunched up his brow. "Something about locusts."

"That the Lord restores the years the locusts have eaten," Frank said. It was not a question.

"Yeah, that was it."

Frank was silent for a time, then said, "I used to think a lot about that passage. It's not the first time Harry has used it on me. I used to think it was pretty much bunk, like how could I relive years that were already gone? But now I think Harry's right. The Lord does return the lost years, but not in the way I thought."

Frank paused long enough to maneuver the car around a thundering truck, then continued in a voice kept quiet so as to not wake the women. "The first thing is that I am forgiven. Not *have been* forgiven—nothing in the past tense. *Am* forgiven now. For all the weaknesses I still have, and the wrong steps I take, and the times I fall. Am forgiven. Freedom from the past, the present, the future, so long as I keep my faith alive and I try to do His will."

Martin watched the animation in Frank's strong features become lit by passing cars. He heard the power of certainty in Frank's words. He felt the confusion in his own heart. And he knew that no matter what else might come, he would never forget the night and the drive and the talk.

"The second thing is a little harder for me to explain," Frank went on. "Now it feels like everything that I have done, all the mistakes I've made, have been molded into something that suits His purpose. God has taken all the times which came before, all the messes I made with my life, and given them meaning. I have handed everything over to Him, and He has given me back a complete new life."

Their time in the Everglades turned into, as Cindy put it, a two-day bug-shoot.

The weather turned unseasonably warm, even for Florida. The trails they followed were under canopies of great trees, which trapped in the heat and blocked out the breeze. Every step drew out clouds of mosquitoes and biting flies. Concentration on setting up shots was impossible. They were too busy swatting at bugs that were trying to turn them into walking buffets. They saw no animals at all.

The second afternoon they returned to the motel hot and tired and drenched in sweat. Mrs. Simpson declared it was time for her to make an executive decision. "For the sake of my sanity, I am heading for the coast."

"Me too," Cindy agreed. "Sorry, Daddy, but I feel as though I've lost five pints out there today. Any more and they might just pick me up and carry me off."

"My troops are deserting," Frank moaned, stripping off a shirt turned wet as a used dishrag by his sweat.

"I'll stick around," Martin offered halfheartedly.

"Don't listen to him," Cindy said. "His mouth says yes, but his heart says no."

"Mine too, if you want to know the truth," Frank confessed.

Cindy beamed for the first time that day. "You mean we can leave?"

"I had so many hopes for this trip," Frank complained. "And it's been a total disaster."

"Not a disaster, Daddykins," Cindy objected. "Just a minor setback. A day sunbathing and restoring my bodily fluids on the beach, and all will be forgiven."

"Angie?" Frank asked his wife.

"For once I agree completely with my daughter."

"Martin?"

"I've taken a total of six pictures in two days," Martin replied. "Maybe they're right."

Frank nodded glumly. "I suppose we might as well leave tonight, then. How much time do you need to pack?"

"Two minutes," Cindy replied. "Less."

"Just let me have time to shower off the swamp," Mrs. Simpson said. "I feel as if strange things are trying to grow between my toes."

A day of sun and ocean at Cocoa Beach restored everyone's spirits. It was still three days until the space shuttle launch, so Frank and Martin went off to see about renting a boat. "Being out of sight of land is one of the greatest challenges a photographer can face," Frank explained. "A calm sea strips away every standard we have. There is no dividing feature, no rise or fall or anything to use as a focal point."

"So what can you do?" Martin asked.

"Maybe you can't accomplish anything at all," Frank replied. "But whatever happens, a day at sea always stretches my horizons. I try to set up something like this every few months, giving myself an impossible task. Afterwards I feel, I don't know, refreshed. It helps me stay flexible. Open."

The fishing port was located down the river-mouth from the ocean liners. To the north, on the river's other side, rose the buildings that surrounded the Cape Canaveral launch sites.

The boat skipper with whom Frank talked had dealt with photographers before. He was a grizzled fellow, old beyond his years, with skin the color of old leather. He wore a battered cap with "Bud" sewn in the crown. His boat was fiberglass and spotlessly clean, about forty feet long, with a high bridge above the cabin. The bridge had a second set of controls, and Martin guessed it was used when the skipper was scouting the waters for fish.

Bud understood that there would be no need for expensive fishing gear or crew. He would take them out the thirty miles or so to the Gulf Stream, putter them around, and bring them back. No problem.

The next day dawned as clear and hot as those before. By eight o'clock, when they arrived at the boat dock, the temperature was already approaching ninety.

The skipper greeted them with, "Don't think much of this weather."

"Why not?" Mrs. Simpson said, handing in a cooler. "There isn't a cloud in the sky."

"Too hot," Bud said. "Too hot by half."

"What is that supposed to mean?" Frank demanded.

"Maybe nothing," Bud said. "Maybe a blow."

Mrs. Simpson glanced worriedly at her husband. "Do you think we ought to wait for another day?"

Bud searched the sky for invisible clues. "Been on the horn twice already this morning with the weather service. They say everything's clear from here to the Carolinas. Shouldn't have no trouble for a day or so. 'Least, that's what they say."

Frank hesitated. "What do you think we should do?"

"Don't see no reason for not going out," Bud replied. "If I did, I'd be calling it loud and clear."

"But you just said—"

"My nose itches," Bud replied morosely. "My nose ain't often wrong."

Frank thought it over. "What are the other boats doing?"

"Going out," Bud replied. "Ain't a one of them worried 'cept me."

"Give us a minute," Frank said.

"Sure thing."

Frank drew everyone back a couple of paces. "What do you think?"

"If all the other boats are going out," Mrs. Simpson said, "and the weather service doesn't think anything is wrong, I'd say we should go ahead."

"It's a beautiful day," Cindy agreed. "Maybe a little wind would be nice, but we can always go for a swim to cool off."

Frank turned to Martin. "What do you think?"

Martin's face must have shown his surprise at

being asked, because Cindy explained, "Everybody gets a vote in this family. Unless there isn't time. Then we do what Daddy says, and jump."

"I think we should go," Martin agreed.

"Just keep an ear tuned to the weather channel," Mrs. Simpson agreed.

"Right." Frank walked over to where Bud stood coiling ropes. "We'd like to go, so long as we're careful about keeping in touch with the weather service."

"The radio stays on all day," Bud said, jumping lightly onto the boat. "Always does."

As the boat left the channel and pulled away from land, Martin felt his fears fade with the excitement of something totally new. Cindy came over and slid her hand into his. Together they stood in silence and watched the shoreline slowly vanish. When the tallest hotel slipped below the horizon, she turned to him and said, "I'm really glad you came with us."

"So am I."

For once her normal frivolous nature was set aside. She stared at him, and said quietly, "Really, really glad."

The hours passed with amazing speed. They swam, they ate, they chatted, then separated at Frank's orders to try and capture the day on film. Mrs. Simpson retired to the cushioned swivel fishing chair at the back of the boat and dared anyone to disturb her.

Martin crouched on the wooden platform off the stern, used for stepping in and out of the sea, and watched the gentle waves rock the boat. The horizon was an unbroken line of sameness. Blue ocean met blue sky in every direction.

Since there was nothing outside to focus on, Martin concentrated on their little world. He photographed the water reflecting the sun. He photographed the ripples running off the boat's side. He photographed Frank as the tall man moved about the boat, searching for possibilities of his own. He photographed Mrs. Simpson in her chair with her book. But mostly he photographed Cindy.

For Martin, the day became a time to observe Cindy with utter abandon. The camera became a second set of eyes, an opportunity to look at her more deeply and more closely than ever before.

He photographed her dancing from bow to stern, following a school of fish that had surfaced alongside the boat. He photographed her laughing with her father. He photographed her stretched out alongside her mom, chatting quietly. He photographed her applying white cream to her nose and lips. He photographed her sticking out her tongue at him, which happened whenever she felt the intimacy of his gaze and became self-conscious. And the more he photographed, the more he felt his heart being filled by the wonder of her.

As they were eating lunch, Bud stuck his head from the cabin to report, "Boat up ahead's hooked onto a big bill." He returned to the controls, started the motors, and pushed the throttles open. The boat crested its bow wave with rumbling power.

Martin looked a question at Frank, who was already reaching for his camera. "The skippers keep in touch by radio," he interpreted. "Somebody not too far away has hooked a fighting fish. Get your equipment ready."

Within minutes the second boat came into view. Bud talked into the radio, got a fix on where the fish was, popped out long enough to point. Frank raised his camera and tensed. Martin followed his lead, then lowered his camera and squinted out over the sun-dappled water. There was nothing out there except open sea.

Then the water in front of them exploded.

A fish as tall as the boat's bridge cleared the water completely. Its bill was a spear as long as Martin's leg. On its back was a fan open wide and spiked with sharp points. Its colors were as rich and deep as the sea. It shook its head in slow motion, then returned to the sea with an enormous splash.

When the fish had disappeared, Martin realized he had stopped breathing. And that he had missed the picture entirely. But all he could say was, "Wow."

"Get ready," Frank called. "He may do it again."

And he did. The sea erupted once more. The fish rose even higher than before, fighting furiously to throw off the hook. Martin was ready this time, and caught the fish at full reach, the sun glinting strong through the back fin.

When the fish disappeared a second time, Frank called, "Can you get us up close to the other boat? I'd like to get a shot of the action."

Bud's response was interrupted by a squawk from the radio. Immediately Bud pulled back the throttles. They turned to see him bent over the speaker, microphone in hand.

The radio squawked once more. Bud slid back the cabin's side window and studied the sky with a worried squint.

Frank called out, "What's wrong?"

Bud did not answer him. His attention remained focused on the horizon. He switched the radio to another channel and spoke into the microphone.

The four of them jammed into the cabin in time to hear the radio answer with rattling static and a voice that sounded like it came from inside a whirlwind.

"Look!" Cindy pointed to the distant boat. A man had come up alongside the person strapped into the fishing chair. The fisherman was shouting and pointing out to where the fish swam unseen. The other man shouted back and pointed at the horizon. Martin turned and searched the sky. He saw nothing but blue.

"He's letting it go!" Cindy cried.

Martin turned around in time to see the skipper reach up and cut the fishing line. The fisherman was furious. He struck repeatedly at his straps, and when they finally released he jumped up, gesticulating wildly and yelling at the skipper. But the skipper was already climbing back up the bridge, heading for the controls.

Bud spoke into the microphone again, jammed it into its holder, and yelled, "We're outta here."

"What's the matter?" Frank demanded again.

"Big blow's out to sea."

"Is it headed this way?"

"Dunno. Got all kinds of crazy reports. But my nose says yes."

"The other boat must think so, too," Cindy said, pointing to where the skipper was wheeling his boat around. The fisherman remained down below, waving his arms and kicking at things.

"Tough call," Bud said. He spun the wheel. The boat canted to one side and turned sharply. "Right now that guy is burning up. Anybody would be. That was a prize fish. But if the blow's headed this way, every minute counts."

Mrs. Simpson asked worriedly, "Are we going to be all right?"

"Soon find out," Bud replied, leveling off the boat on a heading for land and pushing the throttles open wide.

They raced full-out across a placid sea. The only wind was brought up by their passage. The water around their boat was as flat as a mirror. The air felt close, charged with an oppressive heaviness that went far beyond the heat. Martin felt as though he were trying to breathe through a wet rag. He searched the sky behind them, but saw nothing at all.

Bud did not agree. He kept sticking his head out of the window and searching the sky off their stern. A few minutes later his eyes widened from their customary squint, and he shouted, "Trouble!"

The four passengers turned as one. Martin searched and searched, and finally realized that a thin dark line was now separating the blue of sea from the blue of sky.

"What is that?" Frank yelled.

"Cold front," Bud shouted over the engine's bellow. "Big one's worse than a hurricane, 'cause there ain't no warning."

Cindy stepped up closer to Martin and took his hand. He glanced down at her, squeezed her fingers, tried to bring up a reassuring smile. Then he turned back to the stern and felt his belly go cold.

In the space of those few seconds, the darkness had gone from a single thin line to a looming bank of clouds. It was still very distant, yet close enough to see tiny flashes of lightning flicker underneath.

"Coming up fast!" Bud shouted. "Frank, you better get everybody into life jackets. Hook 'em into the safety lines while there's still time."

"Over there," Cindy said, pointing with her free hand. Martin looked and saw to their left another seven or eight boats, all racing flat out for home and safety.

He turned back to the stern and gasped. The clouds were racing up at a speed made even more frightening by their utter silence. The sea around them remained placid as liquid glass. Behind them loomed a beast of rain and wind.

The clouds now started just above sea level and rose up as high as Martin could see. The peaks were crowned by the sun's light, great rolling waves of white. Farther down, however, the clouds became darker, and darker still, and then down at sea level almost black, the shadows broken only by the lightning, which flickered continuously. Thunder boomed out now, as though the clouds rolled forward on great unseen tracks that ground their way through the air. The whole great heaving mass churned and advanced so fast that their boat might as well have been standing still.

"Here, put these on," Frank said, handing them

life vests. He showed them how to unwind the emergency cords and fasten them to the metal cable strung along the boat's flooring.

Martin ran to the stern and snapped a quick shot of a boat behind them racing full-out for safety. A lightning bolt seared down from the approaching clouds just as he hit the shutter. He hurried back to the cabin and gave Frank the camera with hands that would not stop trembling.

Frank gathered up all their camera equipment and stowed it in the under-cabin. The three of them picked up everything that was not tightly fastened and handed it down to Frank. Bud kept up a continual stream of conversation with his radio. He was no longer looking backwards. There was no need. The thunder was now so loud and so close that it rang out over the engine's bellow.

Then the temperature dropped forty degrees in less than a minute.

It was like stepping into a refrigerator. Great wafts of cold air drifted in from behind them on a wind that ruffled the surrounding waters. Little white waves feathered the surface, and the ride became choppier.

The clouds were so close that the upper reaches were no longer visible. In front, all was light and clarity and safety. Behind, only darkness. The rain was a great curtain of blackness that sliced the world in half and raced towards them with terrifying speed.

Frank hustled them all inside the cabin, slammed and bolted the door, closed the windows, rehooked all their safety lines, and showed them how to brace themselves on the chrome bars running just under the windows.

Bud shouted, his words lost in the thunder's roar. They turned and saw that the first high-rise hotel was peaking up over the horizon.

Then the wind rose to a howling fury that whipped away all other sound.

And the storm struck.

Theirs was a world gone insane.

Waves higher than the boat was long rose and crashed over the deck. Bud wrestled a wheel that fought and bucked and sought to break free of his grasp. Twice water poured over the stern. The second time a great explosion of white water and foam broke just behind them, and for a brief moment looked ready to drag them into the deep.

"Should we turn around?" Frank yelled out. "Face the storm and try to ride it out?"

Bud shook his head. He yelled so loud his voice cracked. "Sea bottom's rising here. Waves are nothing compared to farther out. Got to try for shore."

The wind howled with the force of a hungry beast. Martin gripped the railing with both hands and tried not to slip on the wet flooring as the boat rode up to dizzying heights, then careened downwards and struck the wave's trough with shuddering force.

As another monster wave loomed up behind them, Martin realized with gut-wrenching force that he might die.

The wave broke and tumbled down towards them, but before the wall of white water reached them, Bud was climbing the wave in front. Instead of swamping the boat, foamy water poured over the stern. A series of green lights beside the wheel said that the bilge pumps were working at emergency levels, trying to keep them from sinking.

Out of the corner of his eye, Martin saw Frank gather his family up in his arms. The two women clung to him, their expressions tragic. He kissed the tops of their heads, hugged them tight, closed his eyes, and bowed his head.

Martin realized with a shock that Frank was praying.

As the moment continued, he watched and saw a calm settle upon the trio. They clung to each other, and somehow seemed to be clinging to something that for Martin remained unseen. The moment passed, they opened their eyes, looked at one another, kissed again. But the strength of their unseen Friend remained with them all.

Bud shouted and pointed forward. Through the streaming windshield they saw a blinking light rise up and crest a wave, the buoy bobbing crazily.

"Harbor lights!" Bud shouted exultantly.

All of them screamed for joy. Beyond the first light, a second came into view. A few moments later, a third. And with the third, Martin was able to accept that it really was true and not his imagination. The waves were growing smaller. And smaller still. The wind roared in frustrated fury, pushing them now through the breakwater and into the harbor proper.

They were safe.

They unloaded their belongings, totally ignoring the driving rain. The two women gave Bud a from-the-heart hug, which brought a grin to his seamy face. Frank pumped his hand in thanks. Martin followed suit and felt as though his hand had been gripped by a piece of old teak.

Bud led them up the gangway and into the harbor cafe. At their entry a roar of greeting rose from those already present. Another boat's name was entered onto the tall blackboard which usually contained the day's special plates. Everybody stood and sipped at hot cocoa and chattered at once, too pumped up with the passage of danger to calm down. Someone handed him a towel. Martin rubbed his hair dry, then shared a smile and a hug with Cindy.

He slipped over to a back window, away from the greatest clamor, and stared out at the storm-ridden harbor. Life was like that, he realized. Troubles did not come at predictable times. He had had no warning about his father's death. Then this storm had been totally beyond his control. And in both times he had been faced with his own helplessness.

Martin stood and sipped his cocoa and stared at the rain-swept vista, and recalled the calm that had entered the Simpsons' faces. There was no way he could reject that. It was true. He had seen it. They had been given something which he had been denied. And why? Because he had not sought it for himself.

Cindy walked up and asked, "Are you all right?"

Martin turned and looked at her. "Yes." It was his choice, he knew.

"You looked so worried." She slipped her arm around his waist. "We're safe, now."

He nodded. It was a choice he was going to make. He smiled at her, hugged her tight, and said, "Safe and sound."